The Rider in Khaki

A Novel

Nat Gould

The Rider in Khaki: A Novel

The present edition is a reproduction of previous publication of this classic work. Minor typographical errors may have been corrected without note; however, for an authentic reading experience the spelling, punctuation, and capitalization have been retained from the original text.

ISBN: 978-1-63637-496-3

CONTENTS

CHAPTER I

"WILL HE MARRY HER?"

"Do you think he will marry her?" asked Harry Morby.

"Does anybody know what he will do," replied Vincent Newport, discussing their host Alan Chesney, of Trent Park, a beautiful estate in Nottinghamshire, close to the Dukeries, Sherwood Forest, and the picturesque village of Ollerton.

In the billiard room they had just finished a game of a hundred up, it was an even battle but Morby won by a few points; they were Chesney's friends, captains in the same regiment—the Guards—from which Alan Chesney resigned his commission some twelve months ago. Why he resigned was best known to himself; they had not heard the reason; nobody in the regiment appeared to have any idea.

"She's a splendid woman," said Harry, with a sigh.

"Granted, perhaps one of the most conspicuous of the reigning beauties. It may not be a question of will he marry her but whether she will have him if he asks her," answered Vincent.

Harry Morby shook his head.

"She'll marry him right enough. Why not? By Jove, Vin, what a handsome couple they'd make!" he said.

"Yes, but I doubt if it would be a happy union," said Vincent.

"Good Lord, man, why shouldn't it be? They'd have everything they wanted: money on both sides, estates close together, many things in common, love of racing, sport in general, hunting in particular; they're made for each other."

"What about temperaments?"

"All right in that way. No doubt there'd be some friction at times, but very few married people go through life without jars."

"Evelyn Berkeley has had one or two affairs."

"Nothing to her discredit. She's always been allowed to have her head; her father was proud of her in his way, but he was a selfish man, thought more of his pleasures than anything, a bit of an old rip too, if all one hears be correct. As for her mother—you know the story—possibly Berkeley drove her to it."

"Yes, I've heard it. Of course everybody blames her; they always do, the woman pays," said Vincent.

"Marcus Berkeley left her his riches; everything he had went to her. She can't be thirty, at least I should think not," said Harry.

"Is her mother dead?" asked Vincent.

1

"I don't know; if alive she is not likely to come into her life again," said Harry.

Alan Chesney generally had friends staying with him at Trent Park; it was a hospitable house, where everything was done well. His father was a successful man, head of a great brewery firm, a wonderful manager, a staunch sportsman, the owner of a famous stud, and a conspicuous figure on the turf; his death was a blow to racing, his colors were popular, and his outlay lavish.

Alan Chesney inherited his love for horses and racing, but the immense business of William Chesney & Company, Limited, did not appeal to him, although the bulk of his wealth came from that source. It was a disappointment to his father when Alan elected to go into the army, but as he was bent on it he gave way on condition he resign his commission when he died and become the head of the firm. This was the real reason for Alan's leaving the army; there were others also weighed with him. He had the makings of a good soldier in him but "the piping times of peace," did not bring out his best qualities; there was more pleasure than work and the calls of duty were not very arduous for a rich man.

The manager of William Chesney & Company was Duncan Fraser, a Scotsman, whose whole life had been spent in England, the bulk of it with Chesney. An upright, honorable, keen man of business, Duncan Fraser was a tower of strength in the firm. Force of character was stamped on him; he was unyielding when he felt he was in the right, and many tussles William Chesney had with him about fresh moves connected with new departments in the company's procedure. The two men were, however, friends, and had respect for the abilities they both possessed.

It was Duncan Fraser's opposition to Alan Chesney going into the army induced William Chesney to protest against it and give way only upon the stipulation stated.

"He is your only son, and his place is at the head of the firm when you think fit to retire," said Duncan. "He has no right to neglect his responsibilities, and he ought to be trained for the position; if he goes into a crack cavalry regiment he'll never settle down to the work here."

William Chesney agreed with Duncan Fraser, but made excuses for Alan.

"I fancy he considers you will be capable of looking after things when I am gone," he said.

"That's not the point. I'm capable now, but you are the head, and he ought to take your place."

Alan Chesney and Duncan Fraser did not agree well, the

former knew of Fraser's opposition to his joining the army and resented it as an impertinence.

"After all he's a servant of the company," he said to his father.

"And the best servant a company ever had. He's a big shareholder too; don't forget that important fact, Alan," was the answer.

Duncan Fraser was a careful man; he had a large salary, and, being a bachelor, saved most of it and bought shares in the brewery. When William Chesney died he held the second interest to Alan, which gave him considerable power.

To do Fraser justice he always desired, was anxious, that Alan Chesney should be the active head of the firm; but his disinclination for the work threw more and more responsibility on the manager, and although Alan was nominally the head, Duncan Fraser was the man everybody looked to.

Alan recognized this and resented it, although he knew it was his fault.

Duncan Fraser had the tact to handle the situation delicately; he treated Alan with almost the same deference as his father, but did not consult him to the same extent, or take so much notice of his suggestions.

Fraser was a good-looking man, verging on fifty, tall, well-built, an athlete in his younger days, a good shot and an enthusiastic angler. He was a frequent visitor at Trent Park, and to all outward appearances he and Alan were the best of friends; there was a rift in the lute which they concealed.

Alan was popular in the county, his liberality was great, appeals to him always met with a response. His fine commanding presence made him noticeable, his military training had done him good, he was strong, powerful, a good boxer, and no man could ride better. Despite his height and strong frame, he could ride a reasonable weight on the flat, and over fences, and he often mounted his horses and those of his friends. Exercise kept his weight down; he walked miles at a stretch, through the glorious forest, or over his estates.

He had known Evelyn Berkeley since she was in her teens, and when he came home from Harrow, and she was at "The Forest" for her holidays, they were often together; their love for the country was strong and they explored every nook and corner of Sherwood Forest.

When Evelyn Berkeley was five and twenty it was reported, with some semblance of authority, that William Chesney, the wealthy brewer, was anxious to make her his wife, that he would willingly have done so but she refused him. There was truth in this, but the whole facts were not known. Evelyn Berkeley liked William Chesney but she was very fond of Alan, and it seemed to her ridiculous that she should wed the father when she admired the son, although Marcus Berkeley strongly urged her to accept the brewer's offer.

"You'll be safe with him, Eve," said her father. "He's a good sort; he idolizes you. Oh yes, I know you prefer Alan, that's perhaps natural, but he's not sown his wild oats yet and you'll have a long time to wait before you can get him to the post. You're young, marry William Chesney, and before the bloom's off your cheeks you'll be the richest and handsomest widow in the land."

Evelyn Berkeley was very sorry when William Chesney died. He proved a better guide than her father, and her refusal of his offer made no difference in his manner toward her.

Alan Chesney knew of his father's partiality for Evelyn Berkeley but did not know he proposed to her, and the rumors of it had not reached him. He admired Evelyn, but was not at all certain he loved her, and so far had not considered it conducive to his happiness that he should take a wife; he was fond of his freedom, of the bachelor life he was leading, he did many things that would be impossible if he married.

He had a habit of doing unexpected things, and this was the reason Vincent Newport said, "Does anybody know what he will do?" in answer to Harry Morby's question.

Alan Chesney came into the billiard room.

"Did you beat him, Harry?" he asked.

"Just pipped him on the post," was the answer.

"I'm just going to have a look at the horses; will you come?" he said.

"Only too pleased," said Vincent, and Harry acquiesced eagerly.

"Think we'll drive; horses are more enjoyable than motors—that's if you haven't to go any distance."

A pair of beautiful bays were brought round, the shooting wagon was spic and span, almost new, the groom smart and dapper, everything in perfect style.

Alan handled the reins and they drove along the well-kept road in the direction of Trent Stud.

Their way skirted past "The Forest" and as they passed the gates Evelyn Berkeley came out in her motor. Alan pulled up, she stopped the car, and greetings were exchanged.

"We're going to see the horses. Will you come?" asked Alan.

She thanked him, said she had an appointment in Nottingham, and from there had to go to Newark.

4

"You'll be in town for the Derby, I suppose?" said Alan.

"Yes. Are you running anything at the meeting?"

"Three or four. Might pick up a race or two."

"You'll not forget to put me on," she said, smiling.

"Oh no, I'll not forget. I'll call and see you and give you all particulars; shall you have a house full?" said Alan.

"Half a dozen single friends and two married couples; you can stay with me if you like, it will be quite proper," she said, laughing.

Alan did not give a direct answer; he merely repeated that he would call.

"By Jove, she is handsome!" said Harry enthusiastically.

"Not a doubt about that," said Alan placidly, as he touched the horses with the whip and they went along at a fast pace.

CHAPTER II

TRENT PARK

Trent Park was a wonderful place; the house was modern, the new mansion having been built by William Chesney, but the park was full of ancient trees and there were some old buildings. A venerable keep, surrounded by a moat full of water and only reached by a boat, there being no bridge, was not far from the stud buildings.

It was a picturesque spot and many visitors came to see it. History attached to it, romance threw a halo round, there were many stories associated with it, some true, others doubtful, the more doubtful the more interesting. Murder had been committed within its walls in the time of the first Edward; and even down to the Georges; it possessed an unenviable reputation for dark deeds and mysterious crimes.

It was used as a prison in the Tudor times and tradition said many a man had been done to death there without just cause.

Men employed at Trent Park in various capacities reported having seen weird sights: shadowy, wailing figures, mostly women, flitting about, even rising out of the moat where, it was said, bodies had been found, or, to be more correct, skeletons.

The villagers of Little Trent shunned it after nightfall; youngsters were frightened into obedience by threats to bring the moat ghosts after them.

It was a round keep, built of massive stone, the walls ivy-covered, the base green with moss, damp and age.

A massive oak door studded with large-headed nails creaked on its rusty hinges when opened, which was seldom.

A visitor from New York received permission to examine the keep, tower, and moat in search of historical data and facts. He stayed at the Sherwood Inn at Little Trent. One evening he returned from his explorations with a white, frightened face; when questioned he shivered but gave no answers. He hurriedly took his departure and, from stray bits of paper in the fire-grate in his room, it was surmised he had burnt his copious notes about the keep, no doubt being terrified by some ghostly warning to destroy them.

The ruins of a monastery stood at the other end of the Park. A stately pile of crumbling mortar, and stones shifting from places they occupied for centuries. The outer walls stood and inside the square was a keeper's cottage hidden in a warm snug corner,

6

concealed from prying eyes, unnoticeable until the ruin was entered.

A curious place to build a cottage, and nobody seemed to know who put it up or for what purpose the place was selected. It was there when William Chesney bought the estate and it was a long time before he knew of its existence.

Tom Thrush, head gamekeeper at Trent Park, occupied it, living there with his daughter Jane, a pretty girl of twenty, a lonely place for her; yet she liked it and loved to wander in the woods and roam about in the great forest bordering on the Park.

Tom Thrush, for many years, was employed at Chesney's Brewery; it was at his own request he was sent to Trent Park and installed as second keeper and then raised to head keeper in the course of a few years. He was a strange man, lonely, taciturn, passionately fond of his daughter, and spent the bulk of his time in the forest, where he studied wood-craft and the habits of all wild birds and animals. There was something almost uncanny in the way he made friends with the wild things of the woods and forests; no living bird or animal seemed to fear him, and he taught Jane much wild lore and how to make friends with the denizens of the woods.

The preserving of game was strictly carried out at Trent Park and thousands of birds were killed every season; in this Tom Thrush was most successful, a prince among keepers.

The Park abounded with massive oaks, and no doubt at one time had been part of Sherwood Forest, and these were ancient trees that had been spared when others fell. Centuries old some of them, with vast trunks and huge gnarled, twisted branches which seemed to have suffered from terrible convulsions of nature, been put on the wrack, as it were, and come forth mutilated in a hundred deformities.

There were deer in the Park, and white cattle, almost wild, sometimes dangerous, they were confined in a strong ring fence.

One part of the Park was laid out in paddocks for the blood stock, and here the young thoroughbreds from the Trent Stud galloped about and played their games until it was time for them to be broken in and sent to the trainer.

Well-kept roads ran in various directions through the Park, there was plenty of water, a minor river running through on its way to join the Trent. It was indeed a glorious place and Alan Chesney might well be counted a lucky man to own it.

His two friends had gone, after staying a week, and it was arranged they should meet at Epsom for the Derby.

It was seldom Alan Chesney was alone in the big house; many times he wished it smaller, not so roomy, more cosy, in keeping with his bachelor habits. There were parts of it he had only been in once or twice. The long picture gallery he shunned, although some exquisite modern paintings hung there.

When he came into possession he had some of the smaller and brighter pictures removed into the living rooms and the spaces were still left vacant. The windows in this gallery overlooked the Park, in the distance the keep could be seen, and farther away a corner of the monastery. There were large reception-rooms, and bedrooms the size of the ground floor of a small house. The dining-room was oak panelled, the ceiling oak, and it was furnished with massive chairs and a huge table. There was a great sideboard, carved by Gibbons, which cost an enormous sum, carvings adorned the wood mantelpiece over the open fireplace. It was a room in which fifty guests might sit down with ease.

Alan had his favorite rooms, the smallest in the house; his study was a model of comfort, and there was another room opening from it which contained all his sporting paraphernalia. There were guns of various makes, over a dozen; Harry Morby had tested some of them and expressed the opinion that a bad shot might kill birds with such weapons.

A case of fishing-rods occupied one side of the room. Half a dozen saddles, some racing jackets, bridles, dog collars, boxing gloves, foils, whips, boots, spurs, miscellaneous tools handy for sporting purposes.

Pictures of racing and hunting scenes hung on the walls; there was a life-like painting of Fred Archer, the beautiful eyes being perfect, also another of Tom Cannon, Mornington Cannon, George Fordham, portraits of Maher, Frank Wotton and several well-known gentleman riders who were friends of Alan's.

This was the room where guests were wont to congregate and talk over the day's shooting, or discuss the merits of horses and jockeys.

Alan had breakfast, and came into this room to read the papers before going for his customary ride; he was always ready and fit to accept a mount in a welter race, or ride over the sticks in the hurdle and chasing season.

He looked carelessly at half a dozen papers but his attention wandered, he could not concentrate his thoughts on anything he saw, he read bits here and there but they were not fixed in his mind. He tossed the papers in a heap on the table, filled his pipe and smoked dreamily.

There were a dozen servants in the house but he was the only occupant of the owner's quarters. He did not feel exactly lonely, but he liked somebody to talk with, and having been a few days by himself he wished for company.

Evelyn Berkeley was at The Forest and he thought he would ride over and see her; she was always good company and he liked her, but she was dangerously charming and he acknowledged he felt the influence when in her presence.

Why not marry her? He was sure she would accept him if he proposed, and there was no woman more fitted to be the mistress of Trent Park.

More than once he had been on the verge of putting the question to her but something prevented him and he was rather glad he had escaped.

Over and over again he had asked himself if he loved her and found no satisfactory answer.

He knew many of his male friends accepted it as a foregone conclusion he would marry Evelyn Berkeley, and he smiled as he thought how they discussed him and his matrimonial prospects.

It pleased him to think she preferred his society to that of other men, it flattered him when he recalled she might have been a countess had she wished. He asked her why she did not accept the titled suitor and she replied that titles had no attraction for her, that her mind was made up; there was somebody she liked very much, he might ask her to be his wife some day and she would wait.

He rode several miles at a fast pace in the Park before turning his horse's head in the direction of The Forest.

As he was passing the monastery ruins he saw Jane Thrush. She looked very sweet and winsome in her plain brown frock which matched the color of her hair; she had no hat, and its luxurious growth added to her rather refined rustic beauty.

Alan was always courteous to women, and Jane was one of his favorites; so was her father, he had a sincere regard for the sturdy, silent gamekeeper.

"Beautiful morning, Jane," he said. "You love to be out in the sun?"

She smiled at him. How handsome he looked on his horse, and how well he sat the animal!

"I am going to Little Trent to buy a few things for the house. I generally go through the wood," she said.

"You and your father live quiet lives here. Wouldn't you like to be in the village?" he asked.

"Oh no. I love the old ruin, and the cottage is so sweet I couldn't bear to leave it, and I'm sure Father would sooner be here than anywhere," said Jane eagerly.

Alan laughed as he replied:

"Don't be alarmed, you shall live in the cottage as long as you like. Do you ever feel afraid when you are alone at night?"

"No; why should I? No one ever comes here, and there's Jack always on guard."

"Wonderful dog, Jack," said Alan smiling.

"He is. It's three years since you gave him to me. He is my constant companion."

"He's a well-bred dog anyway; these black retrievers are hard to beat."

"If anything happened to him I don't know what I'd do," she said.

"I do," he answered. "I'd give you another in his place."

"That wouldn't be the same at all," she said.

"You prefer old friends?"

"Yes, indeed."

"Then I hope Jack will live a long time to be your faithful companion," said Alan.

CHAPTER III

"HE'S A SPY"

Evelyn Berkeley was at home, instructions were given that Mr. Chesney was to be admitted when he called. She greeted him cordially; he saw she was pleased to see him.

"You bring the fresh air in with you. I suppose you have been riding in the Park?" she said, as she gave him her hand and a bright smile.

"It's the best part of the day for riding. I wonder you do not go out more on horseback, you are a good rider."

"You really think so?"

"Yes—really."

"I have no one to ride with."

"There's me, won't I do?" he asked laughing.

"Oh yes, you'll do very well indeed, but I have to be careful; I'm a lone woman and people talk."

"Let 'em," said Alan.

"That's all very well from your standpoint; you're a man, that makes all the difference."

"Not in these days. Women are taking a hand in most things, giving the men a lead. They are independent; probably they are right."

"Yes, I think they are, but still there are some things they cannot do; women are more likely to be talked about than men, it matters more to them."

"Why should it?"

"Because women are women, I can't give you a better answer," she said laughing.

"I met Jane Thrush as I came past the monastery," he said. "Pretty girl, is she not? She seems to like her lonely life at the cottage, at least she says so."

"A very pretty girl, and a good girl," was her reply.

"Do you see her sometimes?" he asked.

"Yes, very often; she comes here when she likes, Hannah is fond of her."

"You're lucky to have Hannah Moss."

"I am; she's a treasure."

"Been at The Forest for years, hasn't she?"

"She nursed me, that's a long time ago."

He laughed as he said:

11

"Not so very long ago, Eve; we were playmates, I am not very ancient."

"Well, it seems a long time since I was a girl and you a boy."

"We were good pals."

"Always."

"And we are now?" he questioned.

"Pals? Does that fit the case?" she asked.

"I hope so; I trust it always will."

She hoped not, she wanted a deeper feeling to develop.

Alan looked well, such a fine healthy man, strong, athletic, and she loved him; he little knew the strength of her feelings for him, how she longed to be his, to be conquered by him, to feel his strength pitted against her woman weakness. She kept herself in check, there was very little outward show of her love for him, although sometimes it would not be banished from her eyes, and they were beautiful eyes, eloquent, expressive, and this morning as she looked at him the love-light shone there, and he felt its power.

She was a beautiful woman, he would not have been the man he was had he not felt her charm. She was a woman well developed in mind and body, her taste in dress was exquisite, she knew what suited her and declined to be fashioned by her dressmaker. She stood facing him, close to him, and his senses were intoxicated by her fragrance. The scent she used was delicate, the perfume exquisite, it was peculiar to her; a very dangerous woman when she cared to exercise her powers.

"By Jove, Eve, you do look splendid!" he exclaimed with genuine enthusiasm.

She flushed slightly. It was a tribute to her charm and she accepted it; there could be no doubt about his sincerity.

"Do I look better than usual?" she asked.

"You always look well, but this morning you excel yourself, you are grand! I mean it. What a prize for some lucky man to win!"

She laughed.

"The lucky man has not come along yet apparently; I am near thirty," she said.

"At the height of your charms; you'll meet the right man one day and he'll be carried off his feet and surrender at once, he'll have no option."

"Can't he see, oh, can't he see he is the right man! I'd fling myself into his arms if he asked me," she thought with longing.

"He will have to hurry up," she answered smiling.

He remained an hour or so and then left.

"Be sure and come to my house in town in Derby week," she said.

12

"I'll be there. You asked me to stay."

"Will you?"

"I dare not," he said with a laugh, as he mounted his horse and rode away. She stood on the steps watching; at the gate he turned and raised his hat, she waved her hand, and with a sigh, went into the house.

Hannah Moss, at one of the upstairs windows, saw him ride away.

"Drat the man," she murmured, "why doesn't he marry her; they're made for each other."

Eve went for a walk after lunch and her way took her to the village of Little Trent. She was popular with the villagers, the lady bountiful of the district, and gave with a liberal hand.

Abel Head stood outside the Sherwood Inn as she came along, he touched his cap, she stopped.

"We're having glorious weather," she said. "I suppose you are going to the Derby?"

"Never miss if I can help," he replied. "What's going to win, Miss Berkeley?"

"Merry Monarch," she answered promptly.

"No!" exclaimed Abel. "Who told you?"

"That's a secret," she said laughing.

"He's at a good price."

"A hundred to eight."

"I'll risk a trifle on him," said Abel.

"Don't back him because I've told you," she said; "he may lose."

"He belongs to Baron Childs; he's a straight 'un."

"He's as straight as they make them," said Eve. "How's Richard? Have you heard from him?"

"Not lately, thank you for asking. I wish he'd not joined the army; he'd have done better to stay here and help me," said Abel.

"Why did he join?" she asked.

"Got restless, I suppose and——" he hesitated.

"And what else?"

"He was very fond of Jane Thrush," said Abel.

"And Jane did not give him much encouragement?"

"That's about the strength of it," said Abel.

"Jane is devoted to her father," said Eve.

"No doubt about that, but she'll wed someday, and Dick's not a bad sort," said Abel.

"He'll make a good soldier, Abel."

"Perhaps he will; he'll be a fighter, and it looks to me as though there'll be a burst up before long."

"You think so?"

"Certain sure I do; there'll be no peace anywhere until the Germans are licked."

Eve laughed.

"I understood we were better friends than ever with Germany," she replied.

"Some folks will tell you that, but don't you believe them, Miss Berkeley. They're a nasty spying lot, I'd trust none of 'em," said Abel.

"I hope you are wrong, war is a terrible thing," she said.

"So it is in a way, but we've been asleep too long, it won't do us any harm to be roused up," said Abel. "There's a man staying at my place I have my doubts about," he said mysteriously.

"What sort of doubts?" she asked.

"He goes by the name of Carl Meason, but he's a German, I'm sure of it, and he's a spy," said Abel.

She looked surprised as she said:

"What would a German spy find to do in Little Trent?"

"That's more than I can tell; probably he's spying out the land."

She laughed.

"What sort of a man is he?" she asked.

"Not a bad-looking chap, talks well, but there's something suspicious about him.

"Does he speak with a foreign accent?"

"No; speaks English as well as I do," said Abel.

Eve smiled: Abel's English was at times a trifle weird.

"Then I'm sure he's not a German if he speaks as well as you, Abel," she said.

"Now you're chaffing me," he replied.

"Not at all; I am sure you speak very well."

"If he's not a German he's a spy of some sort I'm certain. He's always looking at maps, drawing plans, making notes and figuring up things. It's my belief he's hit on Little Trent by chance and came to my place because it's quiet and out of the way. There's something wrong with him; if he's not German he's in the pay of somebody connected with 'em. I'd bet my last bob he's a spy of some sort, and I'll keep my eye on him," said Abel.

When Abel went into the Inn he found a map spread on the table in the room occupied by Carl Meason. He glanced at it and saw small pins stuck in various places where lines were printed. Putting on his glasses he saw these were road lines and noticed most of them in which the pins were sticking ran from the coast inland; he had no time for further observation, as Meason entered the room.

14

"Rather a good map, is it not?" asked the man.

"Should think so; I don't know much about maps," said Abel. "What's all these pins for?"

"I am a surveyor. I am going through some of the roads on this map; I shall have to inspect them shortly. I came here to do my work quietly. I daresay you wondered what I was at Little Trent for?" said Carl.

"I have been wondering," said Abel. "So you're a surveyor?"

"Yes; I'm considered clever at the work."

"You're a Government surveyor?" asked Abel.

"I am."

"I notice most of the roads you have marked run from the coast inland."

"That's my division; I am doing this for army purposes."

"Oh!" exclaimed Abel. "For our Government?"

Carl Meason looked at him quickly; Abel's face made him smile, he did not look extra sharp.

"I'm not likely to survey roads for army purposes for any other Government," he said.

"No, I suppose not. It must be interesting work."

"It is, very; the more you get into this business, the better you like it," said Carl.

Abel left him bending over the map. When Carl heard the door closed he looked up, a scowl on his face. "Curse the old fool," he muttered. "Wonder why he asked me if it was our Government I was working for?"

He rolled up the map carefully, ticking the place where he had left the pins in red ink.

CHAPTER IV

THE AUSTRALIAN GIRL

Derby week, London hummed and bustled with excitement. Sport was in the air, racing; everybody talking about the great event. There were thousands of visitors in the city; it was easy to pick out the strangers.

Evelyn Berkeley's house overlooked Regent's Park. It was some way out of town, but she found this recompensed by the view, and it was easy to get about in her motor. Alan Chesney called when he arrived in London, before her visitors came.

Conversation turned on the Derby and the Epsom meeting generally.

"Merry Monarch is my tip," she said. "I had it from the Baron; he fancies his horse tremendously."

"It would be a popular win," answered Alan.

"Have you heard anything?"

"The tip at the club last night was Gold Star," he said.

"The favorite?"

"A very hot favorite. I fancy he'll be even money on Wednesday. Have you known Baron Childs long?"

"Some months; I was introduced to him at Goodwood last year, in fact he was one of the house party at Colonel Buxton's."

"Very rich man, is he not?" asked Alan.

"A millionaire I believe; he is very unassuming, I like him," she said.

Alan smiled as he said:

"He is a bachelor, the head of a great banking firm, I wonder he does not marry."

"He has a wide choice, many lovely women would be glad of a chance to accept him."

Alan wondered if the Baron had given a thought to Evelyn Berkeley; it was highly probable.

"The all-scarlet jacket has won many big races but not a Derby; perhaps it's his turn this year," said Alan.

"I hope so, I have backed Merry Monarch," she said.

"I called to give you some information about my horses. I am likely to win three races, so my trainer says, and he is not an over-confident man."

"Lucky fellow, three races in Derby week; your colors will be worth following."

16

"On the opening day Robin Hood should win the Epsom Plate," said Alan.

"That will be a good beginning. We shall all have our pockets filled for Derby Day," laughed Evelyn.

"He's a pretty good horse, make a note of him."

"I shan't forget, no need to write down the names of your horses," she replied.

"The Duke has a big chance in the Royal Stakes; I have a first-class two-year-old running in the Acorn Stakes. It will be her first appearance; she's a splendid creature, a real beauty," said Alan.

"That's Robin Hood, The Duke, and what's this wonderful two-year-old's name?"

"Evelyn," he replied.

Of course she knew it was named after her and she was gratified.

"Oh, Alan!" she exclaimed, "that's splendid of you."

"If she were not a real flyer, with every prospect of winning at the first time of asking, I'd not have named her Evelyn. I waited until Skane pronounced her one of the best before risking it," he said.

"And you think she'll win?" asked Evelyn.

"I shall be very disappointed if she fails. With such a name she can't fail," he said, smiling.

Alan stood near the window; he saw a lady coming up the walk.

"A visitor," he said. "I'll be off."

Evelyn laughed.

"It is Ella Hallam; I don't think you have met her. She's an Australian girl, I went to school with her. She returned to Sydney when she finished her education, and only came to London a month ago. We have corresponded regularly. I like her very much; perhaps you may have heard me speak of her."

"I don't think I have," he said.

"Please don't go, I want to introduce you. She is coming to stay with me at The Forest when the Epsom meeting is over; her father races in Australia, I believe he once won the Melbourne Cup," she said.

Ella Hallam came into the room. When she saw Alan she said:

"I did not know you had a visitor. I ought to have asked. It is rude of me."

"Alan Chesney is an old friend," said Eve. "Allow me to introduce you."

They shook hands, their eyes met, and Ella Hallam felt something in her life was changed from that moment; as for Alan, he seemed quite unconscious he had created any interest out of the common.

"Yes, I come from Sydney," replied Ella, in answer to his question about Australia.

"And your father owns racers?" he asked.

"Yes; racing is his chief amusement. He's always saying it is a very expensive hobby, and exhorts me to economize in order that he may keep things going," she replied, laughing. "He is coming to England. I expect him in about a month. He may bring one or two horses, he was thinking of doing so I know. He has a very high opinion of our thoroughbreds, thinks they are equal to your best."

Alan laughed as he replied:

"I have seen some of your horses run here. They are good, but equal to our best, no; at least I do not think so. I have two I'd like to match against any colonial-bred horse."

"Perhaps my father will give you a chance if he brings Rainstorm," she said.

"Is he a good horse?"

"Rather, he won the Melbourne Cup," she replied.

"Then I shall be taking something on if I tackle him?" he said.

"You will—and you'll be beaten," she answered confidently.

He shook his head.

"I do not think so," he replied.

"Mr. Chesney hopes to win three races at Epsom this week," said Eve. She spoke sharply, she thought they were having the conversation to themselves. It was evident they would soon be on a very friendly footing if sufficient opportunity offered.

"I'd love to see your horses win—and back them," said Ella, still speaking to Alan.

Eve looked at Alan, something in her expression warned him she was not in the best of tempers—why?

He spoke to her, answering Ella's remark.

"I am glad your friend will be pleased to see my horses victorious," he said.

"It would be strange if she were not, especially as she says she will back them—eh, Ella?" said Eve.

"And you? You will back them?" she asked.

"Of course; he has just given me the tips, that is what he called about," said Eve.

"And also to see you," thought Ella.

"What do you think of Mr. Chesney?" asked Eve when Alan left.

"He's a very good-looking man and I should think extremely agreeable and excellent company. Is he an old friend?" said Ella.

"We have known each other since we were children."

"My goodness, how jolly! And I suppose you are quite chums still," exclaimed Ella.

Eve laughed as she replied:

"We are staunch friends. His estate joins my little place where you are coming to stay with me," said Eve.

"I shall have opportunities of meeting him," thought Ella. "You must see him often?" she said aloud.

"Oh, yes; sometimes two or three times a week. He calls when he likes and I am always at home to him."

"It must be ripping to have a man friend like that; no silly sentiment, no love business about it; but he would be blind if he did not admire you, Eve," she said.

Eve laughed. She wondered what Ella would think if she knew how she loved Alan, loved him desperately.

"I don't think love has ever entered into his calculations in connection with me," she said.

"But he must admire you, he couldn't help it," said Ella heartily.

"I daresay he does. He has an eye for beauty in women and horses."

"Couples them together, does he," said Ella; "and probably prefers the four-legged creatures."

"He looked you over pretty well," said Eve.

She blushed slightly as she replied:

"I didn't notice it. Do you think he was satisfied with the scrutiny?"

"It's hard to tell when he's pleased, he takes everything as it comes, but I think he has decided in your favor."

"Do you? That's rather good of him, most condescending," said Ella.

Next day they went to Epsom. There was a party of ten, a merry lot; there was no mistaking they were on pleasure bent and on good terms with themselves.

Eve had a box. She always did things well, and took care when she went racing she was comfortable and had plenty of elbow-room. Alan came into the box after the first race; he was cordially greeted.

"I expect Miss Berkeley has told you Robin Hood is likely to win the Epsom Plate," he said.

"Yes, we've got the straight tip," said one of the party.

"I can confirm it, you can put a bit extra on him, it's a real good thing," he said with a laugh.

He stood close to Ella, his arm touched hers, she felt a thrill; turning to him she said:

19

"What a strange place Epsom is! Such a crowd, and there's no comfort; we're all right here, thanks to Eve, but over there it's horrible," and she pointed to the hill.

"There will be twice as many people to-morrow," he said. "Perhaps three or four times as many; Derby Day is one of the sights of the world, it is never equalled anywhere."

"We can beat you at Flemington," she replied, "and Randwick. Not so many people, but as for comfort, well, you simply don't know what it is here. Where's the paddock?" she asked, looking round.

"Over there," said Alan, pointing in that direction. "Would you like to go? There's more room to-day, it will be crowded to-morrow. It's rather a good paddock, when you get to it, picturesque."

"I should like to see it very much."

"Then I'll take you there," he said, and turning to Eve asked:

"Are you going to the paddock?"

"It's hardly worth while. We'll go to-morrow and see the Derby horses," she said.

"Miss Hallam wishes to see it. I'll just take her and bring her back safely; we shan't be long. Come along," he said to Ella.

"You don't mind?" said Ella to Eve as they passed.

"Not at all; why should I?" was the sharp reply, and from her tone Ella gathered she did mind, and felt mischievous.

"I'll take good care of her," said Alan.

"No doubt," said Eve quietly.

"What a trouble it is to get there!" said Ella as Alan led her through the crowd.

"Yes, a bit bumpy, but they're a good-natured lot, although a trifle rough."

There were not many people in the paddock. Alan pointed out The Duddans and other points of interest.

"Come and see Robin Hood and tell me what you think of him," he said.

"Where is he?"

"Over there."

"Surrounded by his merry men," she said, laughing, as she saw a dozen or more people looking at the horse.

CHAPTER V

ROBIN HOOD'S SPEED

Among the group looking at Robin Hood was Harry Morby. Alan introduced him to Ella, he thought her very attractive.

"He's a beauty," said Ella, as she patted the horse's neck.

"And he'll win the Plate," said the trainer.

"Your team looks like playing a strong part this week," said Harry.

"I hope so," replied Alan, who took the trainer on one side.

"So you're an Australian?" said Harry.

"Yes, I hail from Sydney. I was educated here, at the same school as Miss Berkeley. She has invited me to stay with her at The Forest."

"That's jolly for you, she's one of the right sort, everybody likes her."

"Including Mr. Chesney?"

Harry laughed as he replied:

"We, that is Alan's male friends, think it will be a match in time. They are great friends and much together."

"It is not to be wondered at, she is a beautiful woman," said Ella.

"Very; it is strange she has not married."

"Perhaps she is waiting until Mr. Chesney asks her."

"Pity he can't make up his mind," said Harry, smiling.

"You think he'll win, Fred?" said Alan to his trainer.

"Haven't much doubt about it; here's Tommy, ask him," was the reply.

Tommy Colley was Alan's jockey. He came up wearing the brown jacket, with blue sleeves and cap—the Chesney colors. He was one of the old school, rode with longer stirrups than the modern jockeys, although he had in a measure conformed to the crouching seat. Alan's friends wondered why he stuck to Tommy, some of them considered he was getting past it, but Alan had a knack of keeping to old hands who had done him good service. In business this caused many a split with the manager, Duncan Fraser.

"Like his chance, Tommy?" asked Alan, looking at Robin.

"Very much. I rode him in his gallop, he ought to win; and that filly of yours is a hummer," said the jockey enthusiastically.

"And The Duke?"

"Good, but Evelyn and Robin Hood are better."

"Is this your jockey?" asked Ella.

"Yes; Tommy, this is Miss Hallam, an Australian, a friend of Miss Berkeley's."

"They bring some good horses from Australia," said Tommy.

"And probably my father will have two or three of the best when he arrives," she said.

There was little time to spare and they returned to the stand, Harry Morby with them.

Having seen Ella to the box Alan went with Harry to the ring. The second race was over and the numbers had been called out for the Epsom Plate; the bookmakers were already shouting the odds.

"Craker's horse is a hot pot," said Harry, "there'll be danger in that quarter. When Peet puts his money down he generally has good reason for it."

Peet Craker was a big bookmaker, owner of horses, a heavy bettor on his own animals; he had an enormous business on the course and off.

The horse in question was Bittern, a champion over seven furlongs, he could not quite stay the mile, and he was conceding ten pounds to Robin Hood.

Alan knew Craker well, the bookmaker often did business with him and for him. Sometimes he went to Trent Park. He was a man of good education, there was no coarseness about him.

"Your horse is favorite, Peet," said Alan.

"He has a big chance if he can beat yours," was the reply.

"Ten pounds is a lot to give Robin Hood over seven furlongs," said Alan.

"My fellow's very well."

"So is mine."

"I'll save a monkey with you," said the bookmaker.

"All right, I'm agreeable," was Alan's reply.

Peet Craker looked at him as he walked away.

"Wonder if Robin Hood is as good as Skane thinks," he muttered. "If he beats Bittern he's a good 'un. I'll stand mine, but I'm glad we're saving a monkey."

Alan put money on freely when he fancied his horses, but he seldom bet on other people's. He backed Robin Hood to win a large sum. Having finished his business in the ring he returned to Evelyn's box with Harry Morby.

The horses got away as they entered; a black jacket, white sash and cap, in front.

"Peet's luck's in, that's Bittern," said Alan; "a good start makes all the difference over this distance."

The field came down the slope at a great pace. There were

fifteen horses; in the center was Robin Hood, he seemed to be hemmed in.

Tommy was savage. Not only had Robin Hood been kicked at the post, but also badly bumped and knocked out of his stride when they were going. He used forcible language to the offending jockey, who retaliated in kind.

Bittern liked to make the running, and his rider, Will Gunner, knew his mount well. He had not the slightest doubt about winning; everything was in the horse's favor. Peet Craker looked through his glasses, saw his colors a couple of lengths in front, and lowered them, quite satisfied.

At the foot of the slope Bittern still led, followed by Lantern, Topsy, and Retreat; Robin Hood seemed out of it.

"Rotten luck, Alan," said Harry. "He was knocked about at the start."

"Was he? I didn't see it," he replied.

"He's coming now!" said Ella excitedly.

"So he is!" said Eve. "He has a chance yet."

Alan smiled as he said:

"It's remote. He's a greater horse than I think if he can win."

Tommy Colley's hopes revived. Robin Hood was going great guns, his speed was tremendous. In a second or two he ran into third place, then going on he came behind Bittern, and Will Gunner scented danger. The two jockeys were old rivals, and great friends. Gunner's style was the crouch seat for all it was worth; he often chaffed Tommy about his long legs. The different attitudes of the two were apparent as they joined issue at the distance.

Robin Hood never flinched under the whip, and sometimes required a reminder that a little extra exertion was required. Tommy gave him a couple of sharp cuts, and the brown and blue drew level with the black and white.

Both jockeys were hard at it. Bittern was game, but the ten pounds he was giving away began to tell.

In Evelyn's box there was much excitement, the finish being watched with breathless interest. Neck and neck the pair raced, and the struggle was continued up to the winning-post. Nobody knew which won until Robin Hood's number went up.

There followed congratulations all round. The party had won, there was much jubilation.

In the evening Alan came round to Regent's House and found bridge in full swing; he cared little for cards. Evelyn, who was playing, greeted him with a smile; so did Ella, who sat at the same table as her hostess.

Later on there was music. Ella had a fine voice, she sang well, there was evidence of careful training. Evelyn played as few amateurs play, and as an accompanist she was hard to equal.

"Thanks so much," said Ella. "You play splendidly."

"And your singing is lovely," answered Eve.

Ella received the compliments modestly. She knew she sang well and there was no hesitation when asked. She found herself talking to Alan; Evelyn was distributing her conversation among her guests. She knew how to play the hostess, and it was easy to see how popular she was; the men gathered round paying court to her. She saw Alan and his companion at the head of the card-room and frowned slightly. Harry Morby saw the direction of her glance, noted the expression of her face, and thought:

"Alan's making a mess of it. Can't he see she loves him? He must be blind if he can't. She'll be taking on somebody else just to show him she doesn't care, but she does very much indeed."

It was not a late night. Evelyn said they must be fresh for Derby Day.

Ella bade Evelyn good-night as she was about to enter her room.

"I hope you have enjoyed your day," said Eve.

"Very much indeed. How well you do everything!" answered Ella.

"Glad you think so. Do you know, Ella, I fancy you've made a conquest!"

"I haven't had much time," was the laughing reply, "but I don't mind telling you I'm out for conquest if I come across the right man. I have Dad's permission; he thinks I shall be left on his hands, and I don't wish to be a burden to the poor dear."

She spoke lightly, but Eve thought she meant more than she intended to convey.

"Mr. Chesney admires you I am sure," she said.

"You're quite wrong, my dear; he has eyes for nobody but you. I noticed it when he was talking to me to-night," said Ella.

As Evelyn had seen Alan much interested in Ella's conversation, and never had a glance from him, she had her doubts about this.

"Don't talk nonsense," she answered. "You know very well you occupied the whole of his attention, and one can't blame him; you are really very charming, and looked quite winning to-night."

Eve went along the corridor and Ella entered her room. She sat in an easy-chair thinking over the events of the day. The scene at Epsom, the racing, the excitement of winning did not occupy her; Alan Chesney predominated to the exclusion of all else. From the first he had roused her interest, if not something deeper. She found it easy to tread love's way where he was concerned; she would race along it in her gladness of heart hoping to win the prize in the end. He had already, in so short a time, shown her many little attentions. It was his way with women, but she accepted it exclusively for herself. That evening he had been interested in what she said; she had been frank and candid, telling him freely about herself and it had not bored him. She was in doubt as to how he felt toward Eve. He did not show any special feeling toward her, of that she was sure, yet some men conceal their thoughts admirably. When she came to consider Eve it was different; they were friends, comrades of many years' standing; she was Eve's guest, had been invited to The Forest to spend some weeks. It would never do to come between Eve and Alan Chesney if—if there was anything between them. She hoped there was nothing, but was not sure. She tried to persuade herself Chesney was nothing more to Eve than a good friend, but in this she failed. She was almost sure Eve loved him, and if so she must not attempt to rival her. She smiled, a little sadly, as she thought it would be a difficult matter for any woman to rival Eve in the affections of a man; also she had a conscience, and it was apt to be particular on questions of principle.

It was Derby Day to-morrow, there was no reason why she should not look at her best, so, like a sensible woman, she went to rest.

CHAPTER VI

A FLYING FILLY

A great crowd at Epsom, a Derby Day crowd bent on enjoyment and backing winners. Ella gazed at the wonderful scene in astonishment; it was different from anything she had seen.

It was not a new sight to Eve, and she smiled at her friend's amazement.

"I never expected anything like this," said Ella.

"Is it equal to a Melbourne Cup crowd?" asked Eve.

"More people, of course; but it is quite different."

"In what way?"

"I hardly know, everything is different, the course, the people, the stands, the ring, that seething mass down there," and she pointed to Tattersalls.

"Wait till you see the favorite's number go up, then there'll be something to look at," said Alan.

"Is Merry Monarch favorite?" she asked.

"No, Gold Star and he'll about win."

"Don't you believe him," said Eve, "he's deceiving you; my tip will win, Merry Monarch, I had it straight from the Baron."

"Who's the Baron?" asked Ella.

"A great admirer of Eve's," said Alan.

"Is that true?" asked Ella.

"Mr. Chesney states it as a fact; I am not aware of it," was the reply.

They went into the paddock and inspected some of the horses, but the crush was so great they were glad to return to the box.

Half an hour before the great race there was a scene of unparalleled excitement, for there had been much wagering for some weeks and several of the runners were heavily backed. Orbit came with a rush in the market and touched four to one; Merry Monarch was at eights, a good price, for the Baron was a popular idol with the public.

Nothing, however, shook the position of Gold Star, who was firm as a rock, and Alan accepted five to four about him in thousands; somehow, he was not inclined to save on Merry Monarch, was it because the Baron had given Eve the tip?

The parade was interesting; the new colors of the sixteen riders flashed in the sun, the horses' coats shone like satin.

Gunner was on the favorite. Tommy Colley rode Orbit, Ben

26

Bradley Merry Monarch. He was a great horseman, quite at the top of the tree. His finishes were superb, he had snatched many a race out of the fire—on the post.

Nothing looked better than the Baron's horse as they went past on the way to the post; the scarlet jacket glided along quickly, heading the others. Gold Star and Orbit were much fancied. Curlew, Halton, and Sniper had friends. Postman was the outsider, a two-hundred-to-one chance; only a few pounds went on him for the sake of the odds.

Thousands of people watched the horses, little dreaming that in another twelve months Epsom Downs would be vacant on Derby Day and wounded soldiers the only occupants of the stand, turned into a hospital. There was, however, a shadow of war over the land, and rumors had been ripe for some time that all was not well. Nobody on this wonderful day, however, anticipated the storm would burst so soon. There had been false alarms before, rumblings of thunder from Europe, but the country was lulled with a sense of security which events completely shattered. Hundreds of men watching the Derby were lying dead on the battlefields before twelve months had passed.

The race commenced, and after a roar of "They're off!" the shouting ceased, there was a peculiar stillness for a few moments, then the hubbub broke out again, gradually increasing as the horses came along.

"What's that in white?" asked Eve.

"Postman, a two-hundred-to-one chance," said Alan.

The outsider was lengths in front, his jockey had been instructed to come right away and do the best he could. It was a forlorn hope, such tactics were more likely to succeed than others because they would not be anticipated.

Gold Star and Merry Monarch were racing together in good positions; so were Orbit and Curlew; while Sniper was at the tail end of the field.

Ella thought it a strange uphill and down course, very different from the flat tracks of Flemington, Caulfield, and Ranwick. She would not have been surprised to see a spill at one of the bends, and when Tattenham Corner was reached she gave a gasp as she saw two or three riders dangerously near the rails. Once in the straight the excitement broke loose, the strange, wonderful excitement a race for the Derby causes and which is like no other vast human emotion anywhere, and for any cause. The Derby thrill has a hold upon people that nothing else has, and is repeated year after year. There are men who have seen many Derbies decided and

27

for thirty years or more in succession have experienced the thrill of the race.

A Derby transplanted from Epsom is a mere ordinary race. It is the famous surroundings cause the fascination, and Epsom Downs shares the fame of Derby Day.

Gold Star picked his way through to the front, and as he took the lead there was a tremendous shout for the favorite. It made Ella start, and Eve said:

"Something worth seeing and hearing, is it not?"

"Wonderful!" exclaimed Ella, her face eager with excitement.

Although Gold Star held such a prominent position his victory was not yet assured, for on the right, in the center of the course, came Merry Monarch, and Orbit, with Postman still struggling gamely. They reached the stands amid terrific din, a pandemonium of sound, and people pressed hard on to the rails, five or six deep, in the vain hope of seeing the tops of the riders' heads, and gleaning some information as to the likely winner from the color of their caps.

As they neared the Judge's box Ben Bradley prepared for his famous rush. He had Merry Monarch well in hand, the horse had not yet felt the pressure, that was to come suddenly, in a second. Gold Star strode up the rise followed by Orbit, and again and again he was proclaimed the winner.

But a race is never won until the winning-post is passed, and much may happen in a few strides. Tommy's vigorous riding gave his mount a chance; but Bradley pushed Merry Monarch on, and inch by inch, yard by yard, he raced up to the favorite, joined issue, and a great finish began.

The tumult was tremendous. Ella was amazed; she had seen the excitement of a Melbourne Cup but it was nothing to this. The crowd swayed in masses, the movement dazzled; it resembled a flickering film before the "movies" were improved upon.

Down the course thousands of people, commencing at Tattenham Corner were running at top speed, anxious to discover what had won. Before they knew, the result was out in Fleet Street and the boys were careering toward the City and the West End spreading the tidings.

Bradley's great rush proved effective. He got every ounce out of his mount and Merry Monarch beat Gold Star by half a length. The usual scene followed as the winner was turned round and came back to the enclosure through a living lane, the Baron proudly leading his horse, raising his hat in answer to the deafening cheers. It was the great moment of his life, as it is to every man who has experienced the sensation of leading in a Derby winner.

Eve was delighted, she had a good win. She chaffed Alan unmercifully; he took it in good part. Ella looked at him sympathetically, she had lost her money.

"I suppose you were on the winner?" said Harry Morby.

"No, I followed Mr. Chesney's advice," said Ella ruefully.

Eve heard her and said:

"It's your own fault; I gave you the tip, the Baron's tip—it was worth following."

Next day The Duke won the Royal Stakes and Evelyn Berkeley's friends had another good win.

Oaks Day turned out most enjoyable. The sun shone brightly, the ladies were in force, the dresses worthy of the occasion.

Alan had paid particular attention to Eve after the Derby, and any little jealousy she might have felt regarding Ella was dispelled.

Harry Morby devoted himself to Ella, and they appeared to get on well together.

The Acorn Stakes brought out ten runners, a beautiful lot of fillies, all trained to the hour; but Evelyn stood out from the rest as the gem of the lot and was a raging hot favorite at even money.

Eve wore the Chesney colors and never looked better; all eyes were on her in the paddock as she moved gracefully about with Alan and her friends. From the box they looked down into the ring and heard the cries of "Even money the field."

"The money is being piled on your namesake," said Harry. "She is splendid; and by Jove, Miss Berkeley, you're more than a match for her! You're positively dazzling! She must win—she can't help it. I saw her eying you in the paddock—wonder what she thought?"

Eve laughed heartily as she said:

"So you think she will win. I hope so. Evelyn's a good name for a winner."

"It is, you are always a winner," said Harry.

"I'm not so sure about that," replied Eve; and he saw her glance rested on Alan.

"He's having a wonderful week," said Harry, following her glance.

"Splendid. Don't you think he deserves his luck?"

"Yes; he's a generous, warm-hearted fellow, but in some things he's blind."

"Indeed? What are they?"

"I will not venture to say; perhaps you can guess," answered Harry, laughing.

Baron Childs entered the box. He soon monopolized Eve; it was evident he admired her.

"Better chance it," said Harry to Alan; "you may lose her."

He laughed as he said:

"I can't compete with the Baron."

When the tapes went up Evelyn jumped off in front, racing down the slope at a great pace.

Fred Skane had said it was the best thing of the meeting and he proved right. It was marvelous how the flying filly galloped; there was no fault in her movements. Tommy sat still, letting her run her own race. It was her first appearance and she showed no signs of nervousness.

She lead from start to finish, winning in a canter by five lengths in very fast time; a great performance, recognized and cheered as such.

"It was good of you, Alan, to call such a flyer Evelyn," said Eve.

CHAPTER VII

A WALK AND A TALK

Carl Meason was active, traveling about the country in his motor, waxing enthusiastic over the scenery, expatiating to Abel Head on the beauties of Nottinghamshire.

"Never been on such roads; they are splendid. You can go the pace, there's plenty of room, not too much traffic. I like to bowl along without endangering lives. I'm a careful driver and avoid danger."

At night he still worked at his maps, the occupation being congenial.

"The reason I'm a good surveyor," he said, "is because I like my work; a man never does well when his occupation is against his inclinations."

Abel listened, making few remarks. He had his opinion about Meason and his motoring tours. Letters seldom came to the Sherwood Inn for Meason, he had but little correspondence, his instructions were explicit, requiring no reminders. He seemed fond of the country life, walked in the parks when he had nothing special on hand. His figure became familiar, but so far he had hardly spoken to anybody.

Once or twice he met Jane Thrush and admired her good looks, but was careful not to offend, and had not spoken to her although he wished to do so. Jane took very little notice of people she did not know, but she could not fail to see that Carl went out of his way to meet her. This amused her. She wondered why he crossed her path. If he spoke to her she would not be offended; in the country greetings were often passed without an introduction.

Meason saw her go into the old ruins and wondered what she did there. Once he waited a long time for her to come out and she did not appear.

Next time he was in that direction he went into the place and was surprised to see a neat, pretty cottage almost hidden away in one corner. He wondered who lived there, probably the girl and her parents. He asked Abel about the place and found the head-keeper and his daughter occupied it.

"Is that the pretty girl I sometimes see in the Park?" he asked.

"No doubt," said Abel: "that's Jane Thrush. She's lived there with her father nearly all her life."

"Queer place for a young girl; it must be lonely," said Carl.

31

"She doesn't find it so. She'd rather live there than anywhere; and she's quite safe, nobody would dare interfere with her. Tom's a roughish customer; any slight or insult to his daughter would be resented," said Abel, looking at him in a peculiar way.

A few days later Carl met Jane Thrush going toward Little Trent. He bade her good-morning and she replied. Her tone was friendly. He made advances which she did not resent and said, in answer to his question, she had no objection to his walking with her to the village. Carl was delighted; he was never short of conversation, and he was the man to interest such a girl. He spoke with deference, explaining he was staying at the Sherwood Inn and found it lonely. It was quite a treat to have somebody to talk to, Abel Head was not very loquacious.

Jane laughed as she said:

"Abel can talk fast enough sometimes; you ought to hear him and Father, they are never at a loss for something to say."

"I don't think I have met your father," he said.

"He's seldom out in the daytime; his duties are mostly at night. He's Mr. Chesney's game-keeper."

"That's an important position I should think; there seems to be plenty of game in Trent Park."

"There is when you know where to find it. Do you know Mr. Chesney?"

"I have not that pleasure. Of course you know him?"

"Very well; he is a nice man, so friendly. He gave me Jack," said Jane.

"Who's Jack?"

"My dog, a big black retriever; he's generally with me but I left him at home to-day; there have been tramps about lately."

"Poachers?"

"Oh no, they are quite different, but Father can't bear the sight of such men. He says they are useless vagabonds and will steal anything they can lay their hands on."

Carl smiled.

"I wonder if he thinks I'm one of that sort?" he said.

"He knows you are not. Abel told him you are always very busy making maps, that you are a surveyor."

"So he's talked me over with Abel?"

"Yes; I fancy they both wonder why you picked on Sherwood Inn to work in."

"That's easily explained; because it's quiet, and such a splendid country. I love the country; I came across it quite by accident, I was motoring and stopped there for lunch; it struck me as an ideal place to work in," he said.

32

"And when you are not at work you like to ramble about the country."

"Yes, it is a pleasant relaxation. There are many charming spots about here I have not seen, there is no one to guide me," he said. "That old ruin where your cottage is must have an interesting history, and the keep with the moat round."

"It is, very interesting. I know a good deal about it. Mr. Chesney lent me a book which gives a very good description of it and what it used to be," said Jane.

"Perhaps you will let me see it?" he said.

"I cannot lend it to you, but I will show it to you if——" she hesitated.

"Will you allow me to call and see it?" he asked.

"I do not know whether my father would like it; I will ask him."

"Do, please; I shall be so much obliged. Perhaps he will show me round when he has a little spare time?"

"Father does not take to everybody, but I think he will like you," said Jane naïvely.

Carl Meason felt gratified at this remark.

"Why do you think he will like me?" he asked.

"Because you talk well; he likes a chat with a well-informed man."

"You think I am well informed?"

"Yes; you have traveled in many countries; it must be interesting. I have not gone far from here, only Nottingham."

"No farther, never been to London?"

"Never."

"Would you like to go?"

"Yes, but not to stay there; I do not care for cities."

They were in Little Trent and as they passed the Sherwood Inn Abel Head saw them.

"Well, I'm dashed!" he exclaimed. "I wonder what Tom would say to that. Confound the fellow, he seems to make headway. Wonder how Jane came across him?"

Carl left her shortly after and went into the Inn. He knew Abel had seen them, saw him looking through the window.

"Nice girl, Jane Thrush," said Carl; "a very nice girl, and seems well brought up."

"She is a nice girl," replied Abel; "also well brought up. How came you to know her?"

"Quite casually; said good-morning; she responded. Asked her if I might have the pleasure of walking to the village with her; no harm done, I assure you. What I like about this country is people are

33

so free and easy; it's far better, much pleasanter, don't you think so?" said Carl.

"It all depends. It is as well not to trust strangers. I don't think Tom Thrush would like his daughter to talk to anybody," said Abel.

"Good Lord, why not? Why shouldn't she talk to me?" exclaimed Carl.

"Ask him; perhaps he'll tell you," said Abel.

"I will. She's promised to ask him to show me round when he has a bit of spare time."

"Has she now? Well, I'm blessed! I wonder what he'll say?"

"I'll make it worth his while. I don't suppose he'll be too proud to accept a fiver," said Carl.

To this Abel said nothing. He knew Tom Thrush's failing— love of money. The game-keeper was not miserly, but he dearly loved handling gold, and Abel surmised he had saved a "tidy sum."

As Jane walked home alone, she thought what a pleasant gentleman the stranger was, and how nicely he talked; she never for a moment dreamed there was any harm in speaking to him or allowing him to walk with her to the village. Jane Thrush never knew a mother's care, at least not long enough to influence her life, and her father left her very much to herself. She was accustomed to talk to people she met, tourists, and visitors to Trent Park and the Forest. Intercourse with them broadened her views; she regarded Carl Meason as one of them and he had proved agreeable.

As for Carl Meason, he was eager to meet her again; he had few scruples where such girls as Jane Thrush were concerned, and he felt he had made a favorable impression which he meant to cultivate.

"She's a very pretty lass indeed," he said to himself. "Quite innocent, sees no harm in anything, not even me. I'll beard her father in his cottage; it won't take me long to find out his weaknesses, I'm used to it. I'm glad I spoke to her; she'll help to kill time in this infernal slow hole. I shall be glad when things get a move on. By Jove, if the folks round here ever find out what I am when the business begins in earnest, there'll be ructions. I shall have to clear out quick. There's a lot of risk in what I'm doing but the pay's good and it will be a lot better later on. What fools they are in England! Can't see danger, never suspect anybody."

Jane spoke to her father about meeting Carl Meason. He did not consider it anything out of the way for his daughter to walk to the village with him; he knew she was often asked questions about the neighborhood by strangers; sometimes he showed them round when they made it worth his while; he was always eager to add a few pounds to his store. He had every confidence in Jane; she was self-reliant, not a "silly wench" whose head was likely to be turned by compliments.

"What sort of man is he?" he asked. "Abel don't seem to think much of him anyhow."

"You'll like his company; he talks well, and knows a lot. Abel's not accustomed to a man like this," said Jane.

"It puzzles me what he is doing at a place like Little Trent," said her father.

"He told me he came across the Sherwood Inn when he was motoring and thought it just the place for him to work quietly in," she said.

"A surveyor, Abel says; not much he don't find out," said Tom.

"There's company at The Forest," said Jane. "A beautiful lady, almost a match for Miss Berkeley."

"Never a match for her, there couldn't be; she's the most beautiful woman of her time, and also a good 'un; I often think Mr. Chesney is a fool not to marry her," said Tom.

"Perhaps she'll not have him, Father; he may have asked her," answered Jane.

"I saw him to-day," said Tom.

"Mr. Chesney?"

"Yes; he gave me a present, and there's one for you, Jane. Here it is; he never forgets folks when he has a win," said Tom, handing her a small parcel.

Jane opened it eagerly, then gave a gasp and an exclamation of delighted surprise.

"Isn't it beautiful, Father! How good of him!" And she showed him a small horseshoe brooch set with rubies; it was an exquisite piece of jewelry.

"Must have cost a tidy bit," said Tom, as he handled it tenderly.

CHAPTER VIII

FRASER'S INFORMATION

Duncan Fraser sat in his private room at the brewery in deep thought; no one interrupted him: he gave orders and they were never disobeyed. A stern-looking man, not given to making many friends, yet there was a kindly heart beneath a severe exterior. The manager of a great concern, he was admirably suited to the position, accustomed to handle and make decisions promptly, no shilly-shallying or "wait and see" about his actions. Very few people were aware he possessed unique opportunities of getting behind the scenes, learning government moves, acquiring knowledge beforehand which was advantageous in his dealings.

Information had recently come to him from a valued and trusted correspondent in Germany, and he was considering how best to use it to the advantage of the firm. The heavy taxes on the brewers hit Chesney's hard, but they were able to stand them better than most firms; still he knew there must be a considerable diminution in dividends, consequently in Alan Chesney's income.

It irritated him when he thought how careless the head of the firm was in money matters. Alan appeared to regard the brewery as a huge concern from which he could drain money as freely as beer ran into the casks. He made up his mind to talk seriously to Alan; he had a high opinion of his judgment and intelligence when he cared to exert those qualities. He expected him to arrive in half an hour and knew what to expect. Alan would rush up in his motor, say he had only a few minutes to spare, then dash off again as he arrived—in a hurry.

The head of the firm was always in a hurry; never seemed to have a minute to spare; the "racing rush" took hold of him. Duncan Fraser smiled grimly as he thought how Alan careered about the country in pursuit of his favorite pastime.

"Here he is," said Duncan, as he heard the powerful motor stop, and thud.

Alan came into the room in a hurry. He was not in the best of humors; why the deuce couldn't Fraser manage without dragging him there? He had carte blanche as to how he should act.

"Suppose you'll not keep me long," said Alan impatiently.

"Longer than usual," was the reply.

"Hang it all, I want to go to the races this afternoon. You must cut it short, please, Fraser."

"This is more important than racing; I have just received some valuable information from Berlin."

Alan became interested.

"Berlin!" he exclaimed. "What's up there?"

"War; it will break out before long."

"Who is your informant?"

Fraser handed him the letter.

"Read that," he said.

Alan did so.

"By Jove!" he exclaimed. "This looks serious. Can you rely upon it?"

"Yes," said Fraser, with a characteristic snap of his firm lips.

Alan put the letter down and a gloomy look settled on his face.

"War," he said, "and I'll be out of it, confound the thing! I'm sorry I don't hold a commission."

"I am not. You can't be in the army and look after things here," said Fraser.

"You look after them. It's no use trying to convince me I'm necessary to the existence of the firm, because I'm not; I haven't the governor's capacity for business," said Alan.

"I don't know so much about that; you've never been properly tested."

Alan laughed.

"And have no desire to be," he said.

"I have drawn up some figures; they are formidable. If you agree to my plans, and war breaks out, we shall save hundreds of thousands of pounds. It means a tremendous outlay, but it's worth it; just go into this, I'll be back in half an hour," said Fraser, as he placed some long sheets on the table.

"I'm no hand at figures," said Alan.

"You'll see the force of these in five minutes," said Fraser.

"Then why give me half an hour?"

"Because I want you to thoroughly master them; I can't undertake the responsibility alone."

"Would you undertake it if you owned the brewery?"

"Yes."

"That's enough for me, but I'll go into them to satisfy you."

"And yourself, you'll be more than satisfied," said Fraser as he left the room.

Alan became interested in the figures, which related to the buying of barley, hops, and a variety of brewing necessaries.

"What a grasp of figures he has!" muttered Alan. "Convincing too; I can see it plain enough. Hundreds of thousands saved; he's right—if there's war."

That was the main point—war; and all depended on the information Duncan Fraser had received from his correspondent in Berlin. He was still studying the papers, making pencil notes, when Fraser entered the room. The manager smiled as he saw him.

"You're a wonderful man," said Alan, looking up.

Fraser shook his head.

"You're wrong; there's nothing wonderful about me. I'm a fair business man, I look ahead, and I know my own mind once I see things clearly. How does it work out?" he asked.

"It's splendid, the outlay is enormous, it will be perfectly justified if war breaks out; everything will rise rapidly, and there'll be a tremendous taxation," said Alan.

"What would you advise?" asked Fraser.

"Risk it and buy as you suggest," said Alan.

"There is no risk if you allude to war; it's bound to come. Do you know there are thousands of German spies in this country? There are two or three here in the firm, and they've got to go," said Fraser.

Alan laughed.

"You'll make a clean sweep of them?" he said.

"Yes, and no delay about it. There's——" and he mentioned the names. "Are you of my opinion?"

"Yes; you must give them some reason, they work well."

"They all do, but it's in their interests—I mean the interests of their country. They worm out secrets, they are utterly unscrupulous, nothing is safe from them," said Fraser.

"Then out with them. I say, Fraser, you get hold of some remarkable information; how do you manage it?" asked Alan.

"I pick my friends; I am careful. What do you think that letter from Berlin is worth?" asked Fraser.

"A good round sum."

"A thousand?"

"Yes."

"Then he shall have it."

"You think it is worth that?"

"I do."

"Then we can't be far out in giving it," said Alan.

"You think I am too careful?"

"Yes."

"It would be better if you were," was the answer.

Alan moved impatiently in his chair.

"I don't consider I spend too much."

Duncan Fraser looked at him with a kindly light in his somewhat hard eyes.

"This is a great business," he said slowly, "or it would never stand the strain. Take my advice and cut down expenses; we're in for lean years."

Alan laughed as he replied:

"What an old croaker you are!"

He got up, put on his motor coat and held out his hand.

"I am glad you sent for me," he said. "I shall just have time to get to the course before the first race."

"Would it matter if you missed it?" said Fraser quietly.

"No actual damage would be done if I did miss it. Still, I'd rather be there; I promised to meet some friends."

"Then I conclude you agree with me and will buy?"

"Certainly; it will be a great stroke of business. I wonder if others are thinking of the same thing?"

"They do not know as much as we—yet," replied Fraser.

"Will you join me at Trent Park for the weekend?" said Alan. "There will be no visitors."

"With pleasure," replied Fraser. "I always enjoy a few days at your lovely place."

On Friday Duncan went to Trent Park. Alan welcomed him cordially, although he had half repented asking him: the manager's presence always seemed to subdue everything, even Alan's exuberant spirits. This feeling, however, quickly vanished on the present occasion, for Duncan Fraser was in an unusually cheerful mood and for once in a way left business behind him.

Alan had to meet a prospective buyer at the Stud, and as Duncan knew nothing, and cared less, about horses he preferred to go for a stroll in the Park. During his walk he met Eve Berkeley and her friend, Ella Hallam. The manager saw little of ladies' society, but he knew Eve and liked her; he could hardly fail to be attracted by her.

He went to The Forest with them and remained for lunch. He knew Alan would not miss him, probably surmise where he was. He rather liked Ella, she was unaffected and talked freely on many subjects; when he left she told Eve she thought him a very agreeable man.

Eve laughed as she replied:

"He is a very sensible man. It is lucky for Alan he has him in charge at Chesney's, or I'm afraid the business would be sadly neglected."

"Is Mr. Chesney not a good business man?" asked Ella.

"Not according to Mr. Fraser."

Ella was rather disappointed she had not met Alan Chesney

since her stay at The Forest. She wondered why he did not call; Eve told her he often came.

Duncan Fraser explained where he had been and pronounced in favor of Ella Hallam.

"By Jove! I forgot all about her being at The Forest," said Alan. "I met her in Derby week, a jolly girl; I daresay she improves on acquaintance."

"She evidently did not make much of an impression on you," said Duncan smiling.

"I wonder how long she will stay?" said Alan, half to himself.

"I think she said she was going to London to meet her father."

"He's bringing one or two horses from Australia; he has a great opinion of them; I must try and convince him ours are better."

"Strange how some men are so fascinated by horses," said Fraser.

"You care nothing about them?" said Alan, with a tinge of contempt in his voice.

"No, they have never interested me; perhaps it is because I never had any spare time for them; I've been a worker all my life."

"You despise racing men?"

"Oh no; I think some of them are uncommonly sharp," said Duncan.

"They are too sharp sometimes," laughed Alan.

CHAPTER IX

THE MAN UNDER THE LAMP

"Sorry I have not called before," said Alan, as he shook hands with Ella Hallam, "but by way of a change I have been busy."

"I thought you were always busy," she replied.

"On the contrary, I am afraid I neglect my duties sometimes, but then I have such an excellent manager."

"Mr. Fraser?"

"Yes. You have met him; what do you think of him?" asked Alan.

"I like him. He struck me as a man of strong character," she answered.

"He is. He has a wonderful grasp of everything connected with the firm," said Alan.

Eve entered the room. She said:

"I thought you had forgotten I lived at The Forest."

Alan laughed.

"I'm not likely to forget that," he said.

"My father arrives next week," said Ella. "I have written to him; he will get the letter at Naples. I told him you were anxious to test the merits of his horses."

"He is coming here," said Eve. "I thought it would be nice for Ella to welcome him at The Forest."

"And I shall be delighted to show him round; he will be interested in my stud," said Alan.

"I hear it is one of the best in England," said Ella.

"I think it compares favorably with most of them," he answered.

He remained about an hour, declined to stay for lunch, and Eve did not press him.

He motored to the stud and found Sam Kerridge, his stud groom, waiting for him. Sam had been at the stud since its foundation. He was a clever man with horses, an excellent judge, and a shrewd buyer.

"That American has been here again," he said. "He's dead set on buying Mameluke; I have tried to convince him he's not for sale."

"So have I," said Alan with a laugh. "Perhaps he thinks you can persuade me to part with him; Valentine Braund is a persevering man."

"Like most Americans, he has plenty of cheek," said Sam. "It's a big offer he has made."

"Thirty thousand, and Mameluke's not a young horse," said Alan.

"It's tempting," said Sam.

"I have half a mind to take it," said Alan. "There's Alfonso coming on; he ought to make a name for himself."

"He will. I think he'll beat Mameluke's record," said Sam.

"That will be difficult. What did you say to Braund?"

"Not much; he didn't seem to believe me when I said money would not buy him."

"I'll think it over; it's a big price," said Alan.

He went round the stud with Sam and as usual found everything in order. Mameluke was a splendid dark bay horse, Alfonso a bright chestnut; there was little to choose between them in point of appearance. Alan was very fond of Mameluke; the horse had done good service at the stud, sired many big winners, and he was reluctant to part with him. Alfonso was worthy to take his place as the leading sire. He was a much younger horse and his stock already showed great promise.

The mares were a splendid lot; the best blood in the world coursed through their veins, and Alan never spared expense when he wished to purchase. When he left, Sam Kerridge wondered what had induced him to change his mind.

"He's inclined to consider the American's offer," he thought. "It's a tall price, and I don't think Mameluke, at his age, is worth any more. I shan't be surprised if the deal comes off."

The reason Alan was inclined to consider Valentine Braund's offer for Mameluke favorably was because of the information he had received from Duncan Fraser's Berlin correspondent. He knew if there was war it would make a vast difference to racing, and that the price of thoroughbreds would be considerably lowered. Thirty thousand is not a sum to be ignored, even by a very rich man, and Alan knew Mameluke had seen his best days. He did not care to part with an old favorite, but it was folly to refuse such an offer when prospects, on looking ahead, were not favorable to breeders. He decided to write to Braund and ask if he were still inclined to make his offer for the horse. He did so, and had not long to wait for a reply.

Valentine Braund came to Trent Park next day and said he was ready to pay the money and take Mameluke over when he had made arrangements to ship him to New York. The bargain was concluded and, under the circumstances, Alan thought he could do no better than invite the purchaser to stay a few days with him. This

Braund readily agreed to, and Alan found him a pleasant companion.

Valentine Braund was the head of an American steel trust, and a man of many millions. Thirty thousand pounds for a horse, or for anything he wanted, mattered little to him. A self-made man, he had worked up from a humble position until he piled up wealth beyond his most sanguine dreams. His energies were unbounded, he possessed a never-ending flow of animal spirits, his confidence in himself was immense, he talked and expressed his opinions freely.

Alan could not help liking the man although his manners were hardly to his taste. Braund did not brag, but it was easy to see that he considered money a passport to any society. He was good-looking although his features were somewhat coarse, and his abrupt manner of speaking might have offended some fastidious people.

Eve Berkeley heard the American was at Trent Park; Alan had already described him to her, also told her of his offer for Mameluke. She was interested, thought she would like to meet him. She invited Alan to bring him to The Forest. He mentioned it to Braund, who was eager to accept, and accordingly they went.

Valentine thought American women "licked creation," and said so most emphatically, but when he saw Eve Berkeley he was astonished at her beauty, and acknowledged to himself that he had never seen a woman to beat her, "not even in New York." Alan was amused at his open admiration of Eve; he laughed when Braund said:

"What a woman, splendid! She's a tip-top beauty; she'd create a sensation in New York."

"I thought you'd like her," said Alan.

"Like her! Good heavens, she's past liking, miles beyond it; she's adorable."

"And her friend, Miss Hallam?" asked Alan.

"A beauty, but not the equal of Miss Berkeley, not by a long way," said Braund.

This conversation took place before dinner when they were alone for a few minutes.

"I thought American women 'licked creation,'" said Alan, imitating him.

"Now there you have me. As a rule they do, but Miss Berkeley—she's superb," said Braund enthusiastically.

The dinner was a success; they were lively. Braund devoted himself to Eve, and Alan was occupied with Ella.

"I've bought Mr. Chesney's horse Mameluke," said Braund. "I gave him thirty thousand for him and I don't consider him dear. What do you think of the horse?"

43

"He's one of the best we have, and I am surprised Mr. Chesney has parted with him," said Eve.

"So am I, but then money is money and it was cash down," said Braund.

"Mr. Chesney has plenty of money—I wonder why he sold him?" said Eve.

"You don't think there's anything wrong with the horse?" asked Braund sharply.

"Oh no," laughed Eve; "don't be alarmed. Mr. Chesney would not have sold him to you had such been the case."

"No, I suppose not; but I've known men who would," said Braund.

"In America?" asked Eve, with a merry twinkle in her eyes.

"Yes; there's some pretty cute hands at a bargain in my country."

"But it would be dishonest," protested Eve.

"We don't call it that," said Braund.

"Then what do you call it?" she asked.

"It would be regarded as a cute bit of business. A man is supposed to look after his interests; if another man gets the better of him, it's all in the game. We admire the man who gets the better of another man," said Braund.

Eve laughed as she said:

"I am afraid that is not my way of looking at things."

"No, of course not; how could it be?" said Braund quickly.

Eve was amused at him. He had an unending flow of conversation, his remarks were original, he expressed opinions freely in a way she was not accustomed to hear. On the whole he created, if not an altogether favorable impression, at least a curiosity to know more of him.

It was a pleasant evening, and as they motored back to Trent Park the American expressed his entire approval of the visit.

"Two very sensible women," he said; "also very charming. You're lucky to live here; I suppose you see a good deal of them?"

Alan said he did, and changed the subject. He was not inclined to discuss Eve Berkeley with him.

"We'll go through the village," said Alan. "It won't be dark for a long time, in fact it's light almost all night now."

He drove slowly through Little Trent. Abel Head was about to close the Sherwood Inn; Carl Meason stood near him, full in the light of the lamp, which Abel always lit, whether required or not, at the same hour.

"Quaint inns and places you have in this country," said Braund, as he noticed the sign.

44

Abel recognized Alan and touched his cap. Carl Meason stared at them. As his glance rested on the American he gave a slight start of surprise.

"Who is that with Mr. Chesney?" he asked.

"Don't know for sure; fancy a gentleman down here after buying one of the horses. I heard it was likely Mameluke would be sold; it's a pity, he's a great horse," said Abel.

Carl gave what sounded like a sigh of relief.

"Doesn't happen to come from America, does he?" he asked carelessly.

"Not that I'm aware of," said Abel.

Valentine Braund caught sight of Carl Meason's face in the light; he turned quickly to look again as the motor went past.

"Funny," he said. "Fancied I'd seen that fellow before."

"Which fellow?" asked Alan.

"The man under the lamp. I'm almost sure of it, but it can't be possible in this quiet place," said Braund.

"His name is Carl Meason, a surveyor I believe; he's studying maps, planning road improvements, and he wants to be quiet," said Alan.

When they arrived at the house and were seated for a quiet smoke Braund said quickly:

"I can't get that fellow out of my head—it's strange."

"How strange?" asked Alan.

"He reminds me of a man I had dealings with in America," said Braund half to himself.

"What sort of dealings?" questioned Alan.

"It's impossible of course; what would he be doing here? He reminds me of a man who once caused a lot of bloodshed at our steel works—a strike leader, if not worse," said Braund.

Alan smiled as he replied:

"Such a man would not be likely to remain at the Sherwood Inn, Little Trent, for many weeks. He'd find it too slow for him."

"That's just it, he would; but I'd like to see him again just out of curiosity," said Braund.

CHAPTER X

CARL MAKES LOVE

"I'm going away for a few days. You'll keep my room; I'll be back at the end of the week," said Meason.

"I'll keep your room," said Abel, wishing he was leaving altogether.

Carl Meason left in his motor car. He took the road to Nottingham, which skirted Trent Park, and ran past the old monastery; he slowed down as he neared the ruin and hooted.

Jane heard it and came out; there was a small door opening on to the road.

"Thought you'd know who it was," he said smiling. "I'm off for a few days' tour, but I'll be back at the end of the week. Tell your father I shall be glad if he'll show me round on my return."

"Going away?" said Jane, rather surprised.

"Not for good. Should you be sorry if I were?"

"Yes."

"I'm glad. We seem to be on good terms," he answered.

"Why shouldn't we?"

"No reason at all; on the contrary, I like you. I hope you like me?"

"I do—that is, I think I do," said Jane.

"Not quite sure, eh?" he asked, still smiling.

She shook her head. She looked very charming in her homely dress, her cheeks glowing with health. She was not at all abashed; the self-confidence of innocence, purity of mind, protected her. At this moment Carl Meason was really in love with her; he wanted her badly. It flashed across his mind that he might do worse than marry her; she would make an excellent wife, and not ask too many questions. His look puzzled her; it meant something she did not understand. She lowered her eyes.

"Jane," he said softly, "you are a wonderful girl; I believe I am desperately in love with you."

So it was this caused him to look at her strangely; she understood now. She never doubted what he said; she raised her eyes, they met his.

"Love me?" she said quietly. "Why should you love me?"

"Because you are adorable, lovely, the best little woman in the world," he said.

She laughed merrily as she replied:

"Oh no, I'm not. Father says I have a temper."

"That's not true; you have a very lovable disposition."

"Yes, I think I have. I love lots of things; still that does not prevent one from having a bad temper."

"Jane?"

"Yes."

"Step on the car; let me have just one kiss," he spoke pleadingly.

"No, it would not be right; we are strangers."

"I hope not. I feel as though I were parting from an old and valued friend."

"I'll shake hands with you," she said.

He leaned over the side of the car and took her hand; he drew her toward him; she slipped away.

"Not yet," she said. "Someday, perhaps, when I know who and what you are."

"And if I prove desirable in every way, what then?" he asked eagerly.

"Who knows? You say you almost think you love me; perhaps, only perhaps, I may come to love you," she said.

He thought it not advisable to press her farther; he had made good headway, she was prepossessed in his favor, that was evident from her manner. He shook her hand again, then started the car; as he went round a bend in the road he turned and waved to her; she responded, then went inside and shut the gate. She sat down on a seat in the garden; the smile on her face betokened pleasant thoughts.

Carl Meason stopped the car at a well-known hotel facing the Market Place; he had been there before. From the orders he gave it appeared he had no intention of going on that day at any rate. He took his dispatch box to his room; he always carried it, never trusted it to anybody.

"You can bring my bag to my room at once," he said as he passed through the hall and went upstairs. When the hall porter put it down he was about to unstrap it.

"Never mind that; I'll do it," said Carl, handing him a tip.

He locked the door and opened his case, taking out some letters and several newspaper cuttings, which he proceeded to read carefully.

"It's Valentine Braund right enough," he muttered. "What the deuce brings him to Trent Park? Buying a horse, that's one reason. Wonder if he heard I was at Little Trent? Don't see how he could as I'm not sailing under my own name. Better perhaps if I'd not given Carl, but it's far enough from Karl Shultz to be safe. He'd like to have me laid by the heels, but he has no evidence to go upon. I got out of that mess well. It was a blow up and no mistake; nearly a hundred killed, and double the number injured. It had to be done; it frightened him and a lot more; there's several men hate me like poison over that job. They suffered while I got off free and had most of the money. Wonder if he recognized me? Don't think so; he'd never expect to come across me in such a place. Much better go away until the coast's clear. He'll not stay at Trent Park long."

He placed the letters and papers in his bag again. More than once he had made up his mind to destroy them, but something stayed his hand; they were dangerous if discovered but this was not likely to happen.

His thoughts turned to a more pleasant subject—Jane Thrush. Utterly unscrupulous though he was, even Carl Meason, as he chose to style himself, had some hesitation in plotting her downfall. She fascinated him. The women who had come into his life were totally different from her; there wasn't a point of resemblance. It was her innocence, her pure country charms, held him spellbound. Many women had helped him in his nefarious designs; they fell easy victims to his blandishments and his payments. He found them useful; one woman in particular had proved invaluable in the case of the great explosion at the Valentine Steel Works. It was Mannie Kerrnon who actually carried out his designs. He had some of her letters in his case. There was no love between them, there had been none between them; she reaped her reward in money, which she much preferred to affections.

Mannie Kerrnon was an Irishwoman on the mother's side. Her father was a blackmailer, a despicable ruffian, in the pay of a notorious New York Inspector of Police. She suspected him of killing her mother and she hated him as a murderer. It was mainly because her father, Dirk Kerrnon, was employed at the Valentine Steel Works that she undertook to help Carl Meason in his nefarious plot. It was a sad disappointment when Dirk Kerrnon escaped with a few scratches; he never suspected his daughter's hand in the affair. He entered the steel works in order to spy on Valentine Braund. The Inspector had given him some useful hints to go upon, but Braund was a careful man and more than a match for half a dozen Kerrnons.

After the affair Mannie Kerrnon quarreled with Carl Meason over the money due to her. She was outwitted and, being the woman she was, she intended being revenged on him. So far she had not succeeded, nor had she any idea where he was, or what he was doing; and he had no intention of enlightening her if he could help it. He was safe as regards the great explosion at the steel works. She could not "split" on him without compromising herself.

As Meason sat in his room at the hotel his mind went back to the old days in New York, when he was hand and glove with the biggest set of sharks in the city, and a pliable tool of Tammany when well paid for his nasty work. What little conscience—and most men have some stored away—he possessed revolted at his intentions toward Jane Thrush—not that they were entirely dishonorable, but he knew a man with such a past and present as his had no right to pollute the life of any bright, happy, innocent woman. To be troubled with scruples was new to him; he had sent innocent men to death without a tremor, had even seen men and women go to long terms of imprisonment through his instrumentality, and thought nothing of their misery; and here he was actually hesitating about sacrificing Jane Thrush on the altar of his desires. Marry her, he even went so far as to declare he would, and was astounded at his honest intentions; he actually laughed, but it was uneasily.

He went out, walked about; at night he turned into a music hall, but variety turns did not interest him; he could not raise a laugh and returned to the hotel by ten o'clock. Jane's face haunted him; no woman had ever so obsessed him. It made him angry that he, Carl Meason, should be caught in the toils, discover that a woman had a hold over him.

Gradually he pushed her into the background and thought over the work he had in hand. It was of great importance and dangerous. When war came he might be shot at any time if his doings were discovered. He was accustomed to dangers; many times had he risked his life; bad though he was, there was nothing cowardly about him. He had some contempt for death, although he dearly loved life. There are bad men who are brave, and such was he—brave, that is, in so far as he cared little for risks so long as he reaped rewards.

He passed a restless night. When he sank into a troubled sleep he imagined he was laid by the heels and about to be shot suddenly. In some unaccountable way Jane rushed up as the soldiers were about to fire, with a reprieve. He awoke quivering with joyful excitement at being saved from sudden death. It gave him an appetite for breakfast.

The Nottingham Guardian was perused; from it he learned that Valentine Braund, the American steel magnate, had purchased Mr. Alan Chesney's famous horse, Mameluke, for thirty thousand pounds and his destination was New York. He was more interested in reading that Mr. Braund had been Mr. Chesney's guest at Trent Park for a few days and was returning to London on Saturday.

"That suits me," said Carl to himself. "I'll get back to Little Trent that day; I'll drop a note to surly Abel and advise him."

Before noon he motored to Derby; from there he went to Haddon Hall and Chatsworth. He was fond of beautiful scenery and Derbyshire pleased him. He was, however, more familiar with Norfolk and the coast towns; roads running from the coast interested him and he knew most of them from Hunstanton as far north as Scarborough. He was later to make sinister use of the knowledge.

CHAPTER XI

THE BARON'S TIP

War clouds were gathering when the royal meeting began at Ascot, but very few people imagined they would burst so soon.

Alan Chesney had a strong team for the fashionable gathering; and, as usual. Eve Berkeley had taken a house at Ascot, among her guests being Ella Hallam, Harry Morby, and Vincent Newport, also Bernard Hallam, who had just arrived from Australia. Alan stayed at the Royal Hotel, where his horses were stabled. In the team were the Epsom winners, Robin Hood, The Duke, and Evelyn; in the Hunt Cup he had Bandmaster, with the light weight of seven stone.

Fred Skane pronounced Bandmaster a pretty good thing for the popular handicap; he was much surprised when the horse only had seven stone allotted him.

It was a brilliant Ascot; it always is, but on this occasion there seemed to be more people than usual, and there was much gaiety in the neighborhood.

Eve Berkeley, however, did not seem in such high spirits as usual. Her love for Alan Chesney grew and strengthened. She longed for him to ask her to be his wife, and wondered why he hung back. Was it possible he did not see how she loved him? Alan had not been to The Forest much lately, and she wondered why. Her attachment to him caused her pain, for she saw no signs that it was returned in the way she desired. Had she offended him in any way? She was not aware of having done so! Her surroundings at Ascot, however, dispelled these gloomy feelings before the first day's racing was over, and Alan had been more attentive to her than for some time past.

On Hunt Cup Day there was a tremendous crowd, and thirty runners were saddled for the big race. Spur was favorite, and even in such a big field he touched four to one an hour before the race. Another well backed was Manifest, while Hooker, Bird, and half a dozen more had plenty of friends. Bandmaster stood at a hundred to five in the betting, and at this price Alan and his friends secured some good wagers.

Bernard Hallam was impressed by the horses, and his remarks in the paddock proved he was a good judge. The Australian had a free and easy way that soon won him friends. He was more approachable than Valentine Braund, although they seemed to have much in common.

He was delighted with Eve Berkeley, and told his daughter she was the most beautiful woman he had seen.

"Don't fall in love with her," laughed Ella; "she's dangerous, has a host of admirers, but it doesn't make her a bit conceited. She is my best friend; I like her so much."

Eve got on well with Bernard Hallam; he amused her. She liked him better than the American; she thought him more genuine and reliable.

Baron Childs was running White Legs in the Hunt Cup, a five-year-old chestnut with four white legs, a useful horse, winner of three or four good handicaps. He was talking to Eve Berkeley in the paddock as Alan Chesney went across to Bandmaster. Eve did not see him; she was in animated conversation. Alan smiled as he saw them, wondering if she was requesting another tip, and if it would prove as good as Merry Monarch.

"Not half a bad horse," said Bernard Hallam as he looked at Bandmaster.

"He's pretty good and he's got a very light weight. I fancy he'll just about win," said Alan.

Harry Morby and Vincent Newport had already backed the horse and were enthusiastic about his chances. Valentine Braund pronounced Bandmaster too light and said he would look elsewhere for the winner.

"Better ask Miss Berkeley for the tip. She's talking to Baron Childs—he owns White Legs," said Alan.

"Not a bad idea," replied Braund. "Do you really think your horse has a chance?"

"Of course I do; I've backed him."

"Scraggy animal, not my sort at all."

"Sorry he does not please you," said Alan, laughing; "but your poor opinion will not stop him."

Skane was saddling the horse. Mark Colley, Tommy Colley's youngest brother, stood close by. He was to ride, and had already donned the brown and blue-sleeved jacket. Mark was a clever lightweight, and had been well coached by his brother and Fred Skane, whose apprentice he was, but he had already forfeited the five pound allowance, having ridden the requisite number of winners. He was a merry little fellow, and still retained his boyish ways, although Skane said he had the wisdom of a man in his head. His brother, Tommy, was riding Manifest, and Ben Bradley had the mount on White Legs.

Half an hour before the horses went out there was a gay scene in the paddock, animated conversations were going on, many tips were given, and the interest in the race was intense.

Baron Childs was confident about White Legs; the horse had been highly tried, and Ben Bradley was sanguine of winning.

"You gave me the Derby winner," said Eve, "and I shall back your colors again to-day."

"Mr. Chesney's horse must have a good chance; he has a very light weight," said the Baron.

"I believe he thinks it is a good thing; but he said Gold Star would win the Derby and that did not come off," said Eve.

"Do you like my horse?" he asked.

"Very much. He is in splendid condition."

"Then back him. I feel sure it will bring luck to my colors."

"Have you met Mr. Hallam?" she asked. "He has recently come from Australia, and is well known in the racing world there."

"I should like to meet him."

"Then I will introduce you; he is over there looking at Bandmaster," said Eve, and they walked in that direction.

"Here comes Eve with her escort," said Alan, laughing.

"The Baron evidently enjoys her society," said Ella. Then as Eve joined them she said:

"Has Baron Childs given you another tip?"

"Yes, White Legs; I shall back him," answered Eve, and then introduced Mr. Hallam, who at once monopolized the Baron's attention.

"So you are going to back the Baron's tip again?" said Alan.

"Yes. Why not?"

"Because I think my horse will win," said Alan.

"Very well then; I will stick to White Legs," said Eve.

"Quite right, follow the Baron; it was a favorite cry years ago," was Alan's reply.

"You do not appear to care whether I back your horse or not," said Eve sharply.

"I don't suppose it will make any difference to his winning chance," said Alan.

"The Baron says I bring him good luck when I back his horses," she replied.

"Very nice of him, I am sure. I suppose he puts Merry Monarch's Derby win down to that cause."

"Perhaps he does; anyhow he's more complimentary than you," snapped Eve.

Alan was amused. What was she cross about?

Eve saw he was amused and it irritated her. She began to think he cared very little about her; this feeling hurt and caused her pain mingled with anger. Why was he so blind when others acknowledged her charms, sometimes made love to her; she had spurned them all for his sake and he neglected her. She felt reckless; a plunge might relieve the tension, cause excitement, make her forget these things. She turned to the Baron and said:

"Will you execute a commission for me?"

"With pleasure. Are you going to back my horse?"

"Yes; put me five hundred on," she said.

He thought it a large sum but made no remark except to say she might consider it done.

"I will get the best price possible," he said, "and I hope he will win."

"So do I," she replied.

Alan overheard this; she intended he should, and when the Baron left he said:

"You have backed the wrong horse this time; the Baron will not win."

"I suppose you think I ought to have backed your horse because you are my next-door neighbor?" she answered sharply.

He laughed.

"Most of your friends are on Bandmaster."

"Then I shall be able to chaff them when White Legs has won," she answered.

"I say, old man, your horse is coming with a rattle in the betting; there's a pot of money going on," said Harry Morby.

"Mine, no doubt," answered Alan. "I have sent out a late commission. I am anxious to win; it will take Miss Berkeley down a peg; she always pins her faith to the Baron's colors."

"That's your fault," said Harry.

"Why?"

"Because you treat her with indifference and she doesn't deserve it."

"I am not aware of doing so," said Alan. He would have resented this from anybody except Morby, who was a privileged person.

Captain Morby did not pursue the subject further.

"You can keep a secret, Alan?" he asked.

"I'll try. You're a mysterious fellow, Harry."

"It's about the regiment," he said. "We're to hold ourselves ready at a moment's notice—don't split—I might be court-martialled."

"Whew!" whistled Alan. "This looks serious."

"Bet you there's war before long; it's a bigger cert than Bandmaster," said Harry.

"And I'm out of it."

"You needn't be. Join us again. You'll easily get your

commission; they'll want all the men they can get, especially officers."

"If there is trouble I shall not be idle," said Alan.

"I know that, old fellow; no need to tell me that."

Something seemed to be in the air. There were many officers present and they were talking in groups of three or four. Judging by their faces it was not about racing; Alan noticed this and thought:

"It's coming, the great upheaval; Fraser's man is right. By Jove, I'll hustle, as Braund would say, when things begin to move."

The horses were going to the post and the June sun shone on the thirty bright jackets as they went past. The din in Tattersalls was deafening. In the crowded enclosure there was hardly room to move; eager backers jostled each other in their anxiety to get at the bookmakers.

Peet Craker left the rails for a moment as he saw Alan Chesney.

"I've a matter of a couple of thousand left against Bandmaster," he said.

"I'll have it," answered Alan; and the bookmaker said, "at a hundred to eight."

"That's a fair price," said Alan.

"Will he win, Mr. Chesney?"

"He has a real good chance, Peet," replied Alan.

The horses disappeared over the brow of the hill, cantered down the slope, and ranged behind the barrier, with the trees for a background. It was a beautiful line of color as seen from the top of the stands.

CHAPTER XII

A FINE FINISH

The big field got away in an almost unbroken line, a splendid start; a loud shout proclaimed the race had commenced. For a few minutes they disappeared, then as they came up the rise the caps appeared over the brow of the hill, and in a couple of seconds the thirty horses were in full view, stretched across the wide course, advancing like a cavalry charge.

A wonderful race the Royal Hunt Cup, a beautiful sight. It has been described scores of times and no description exaggerates its charm. The course is grand, the surroundings picturesque; historical associations cling to the famous heath, where kings and princes, lords and commoners, have assembled year after year, and royal processions have come up the course amid the enthusiastic plaudits of vast crowds. Truly the sport of racing is the sport of kings, and no less of a huge majority of the people.

Bernard Hallam and Valentine Braund acknowledged its charm. There was nothing quite like it anywhere, one of the racing sights of the world, different from Epsom on Derby Day, Doncaster on Leger Day, or glorious Goodwood, unique in its way; no such gathering can be seen in any other country.

The attention of thousands of people was riveted on the horses; all other thoughts were excluded. For a few brief moments everything was forgotten but the business in hand, the probable result, which horse would be added to the long roll of Hunt Cup winners.

The thirty horses were almost level as they came in sight, one or two stragglers, but it was an even race so far. As they began the ascent, the stiff pull to the winning-post, the field lengthened out, horse after horse fell back, and a dozen only possessed chances. The rise finds out the weak spots, and the lack of a final gallop makes a lot of difference. It takes a good horse to win a Hunt Cup; no matter if he does little after, he must be brilliant on the day.

Alan stood with Captain Morby and Captain Newport high on the grand-stand. They knew where to command the best view of the race; it was a climb, a scramble to get there, but worth it.

"Bandmaster's in the center," said Harry. "He's going strong, but he'll have to make his run soon, there's a good many lengths between him and Spur."

The favorite was at the head of the field, traveling in great style. There was just a suspicion he would not quite stay the course, but he seemed to be giving it the lie. Close on his heels came Manifest, Bird, Hooker, Peter's Lad, Beltan, and White Legs.

The Baron's horse began slowly, but soon joined up with the rest. The scarlet jacket was prominent, and as Eve saw it creeping toward the front, she felt confident the Baron's tip would again come off. She wondered why she did not feel enthusiastic at the prospect of a good win. Was it because she would rather have had her money on Bandmaster and see Alan's colors successful? Perhaps it was; anyhow it was absurd to wish to see his colors in front when her money was on White Legs.

Manifest shot to the front as they drew level with the lawn, followed by Bird, and Peter's Lad; with a rush came Scout, an outsider. White Legs was gaining ground. Right in the center of the course was Bandmaster, who liked the stiff going and tackled the work like a good 'un, the seven stone gave him every chance.

Alan was anxious to win; the Hunt Cup was a race he often had a shot at; so far his horses had not run into a place. He had great hopes of Bandmaster's changing his luck.

Valentine Braund backed Manifest, not a bad pick; Bernard Hallam was on Bandmaster; so was Ella, and most of Eve Berkeley's party followed the brown and blue sleeves.

A loud shout greeted the appearance of White Legs in the leading trio, and Bradley looked so much at ease that all who had backed the horse were confident; before the distance was reached the scarlet jacket held the lead, and the Baron's horse appeared to have a mortgage on the race.

Young Colley still had Bandmaster in the center of the track, clear of the others. He was riding a cool, well-judged race, and had every confidence in his mount. Yard by yard the horse crept up; his jockey knew he was gaining at every stride. He measured the distance to the winning-post with critical eyes and felt certain of victory. From the stands Bandmaster seemed to be a long way behind the leaders, and Alan thought his bad luck in the race was to continue. Gradually the sounds increased until they culminated in a roar as White Legs came on at the head of the field, followed by Manifest, and Spur, who had come again in gallant style.

A lull in the shouting for an infinitesimal moment, then a terrific roar proclaimed Bandmaster was pulling hard.

The brown and blue came along fast, very fast, and there was no sign of faltering on the part of Bandmaster, who tackled his stiff work in bull-dog style.

"By gad, he'll do it!" exclaimed Harry excitedly.

"Looks cheerful," said Vincent.

Alan made no remark. He was not quite certain his horse would catch White Legs and Manifest; he had given Spur the go by.

There was considerable doubt as to which horse would win, although the odds were in favor of White Legs.

Bradley, riding a confident race, was on the alert; he never threw a chance away. Tommy Colley got every ounce out of Manifest; and when his brother drew alongside on Bandmaster he knew he must make the last ounce a trifle over weight to win.

For a second the pair hung together, then Manifest was beaten, but struggled on. Roar upon roar came from the vast crowd as Bandmaster got to White Legs' quarters, and the excitement was tremendous.

Eve Berkeley looked on anxiously. At this critical point she hoped the Baron's horse would be first past the post; she would draw a large sum, and the prospect of winning was delightful.

Bradley was the stronger rider, but he had not more determination than his young rival. Bandmaster drew level, and in the next few strides got his head in front. At this Alan's feelings grew too strong for him and he shouted:

"Bandmaster wins!" two or three times.

It was a grand race and one to be remembered.

Again White Legs held a slight advantage, but Bandmaster was not done with, and the difference in weight told its tale. Colley was riding hard; it was a very clever effort on his part, and recognized as such. As they closed on to the winning-post Bandmaster again got his head in front and this time White Legs could not wrest the advantage from him.

A few more strides decided the race. Bandmaster won by half a length from White Legs, with Manifest third.

Although Alan's horse started at twelve to one he was heavily backed, and his win was well received. There was much cheering as the horse came in; the brown and blue was popular; the Chesney colors were always out to win.

Alan came in for a full share of congratulations, Baron Childs being one of the first to greet him.

"I suppose I must join in the paeans of victory," said Eve smiling.

"You can't feel very delighted under the circumstances," said Alan. "It would have suited you better had White Legs won."

"Perhaps it would. Still I am very glad you have won a Hunt Cup at last; you have had several tries," she replied.

"It's good of you to say so," he said. "I told you my horse had a big chance."

"You did. I don't know what made me follow the Baron's tip."

"I think I do."

"What?"

"You have more confidence in his advice than mine," he said.

"I do not think that was the reason."

"What other could there be?"

"Obstinacy," she said.

"I never thought of that—perversity would be better."

"Much the same thing," she replied.

"I am afraid I put you wrong," said the Baron. "If it had not been for me you would no doubt have backed Mr. Chesney's horse."

"You must not blame yourself for that. I am quite satisfied," she said.

"You would have been more satisfied had the Baron's horse won," said Alan.

"Naturally; I backed it."

"Not for that reason alone," answered Alan, as he walked away and joined Ella and her father.

"He leaves me for Ella always," thought Eve with a pang, "and yet I do not think he cares for her that way. I believe he half loves me. I'll put him to the test one of these days, it's worth the risk; nothing venture, nothing have—an old saying which often comes true."

When Alan returned to Trent Park he found Duncan Fraser waiting for him and at once knew there was something important to communicate. Fraser looked serious as he said:

"I hope you had an enjoyable time at Ascot?"

"Yes; won the Hunt Cup and another race. Made a few thousands in the meeting," said Alan.

"There'll be war in little over a month," said Fraser.

"You have had more news from Berlin?"

"This letter came this morning. I knew you were to be home to-day, so thought I'd bring it over."

Alan thanked him, read it, and said:

"What on earth is the Government doing? It ought to be informed."

"It is—has been for sometime. But we know how it is. They always wait until their hands are forced—they are afraid."

"Of what, of what can a British Government be afraid?"

"First and foremost, of the anti-war party, the peace-at-any-price men; then the labor party, votes are the chief consideration. It's abominable," said Fraser.

"Like sticking to office, I suppose?"

"Yes; at all costs."

"You are certain they know there will be war?"

"They must."

"And they will meet the shock unprepared?"

"As regards the army, yes; not the navy. There never was a navy stronger than ours at the present day, but it's been a tremendous fight to get the money, men and ships," said Fraser.

"You ought to be in the House," said Alan.

Fraser laughed.

"I should want a free hand from my constituents," he said.

"And you'd get it; you're just the man," replied Alan.

"What are you going to do?" asked Fraser.

"If war breaks out?"

"Yes."

"Try and get the commission I threw up," said Alan.

"I thought so, and really I can't blame you; we shall want every man we can get," said Duncan Fraser.

CHAPTER XIII

ALAN IS BLIND

It was about a month later when Alan called at The Forest and found Eve Berkeley alone. Ella was with her father in London; they had accepted her invitation to pay another visit later on. She had been waiting for him, wondering why he did not call. She soon heard the reason.

"I have been awfully rushed," he said. "Lots of things to see to at Chesney's before I go away."

"Go away!" she exclaimed. "Where are you going? This is rather sudden; I am surprised."

"I have joined the army again. I have been fortunate enough to get a commission as captain. I tried hard to get back in my old regiment, but there was no vacancy. I shall be gazetted to the 'Sherwoods' in a few days; they are at Derby now. There are stirring times ahead, and I'm not sorry. It was bound to some sooner or later."

"What?"

"War."

She looked incredulous.

"Are you sure? What makes you so certain?"

"Fraser has a reliable man in Berlin; he sent the information. We have acted upon it—in the brewery—and I did not mean to wait weeks for a chance when war is declared," he said.

"Duncan Fraser seems to be a valuable mine of information," she said.

"He is. Do you know, he's a wonderful man, Eve."

She laughed as she replied:

"Your father always had a high opinion of his abilities."

"You and my father were jolly good friends."

"We were on excellent terms; I liked him."

"He could be very agreeable when he chose."

"And in that respect his son resembles him."

Alan laughed.

"Then I suppose you do not think I always choose to be agreeable?" he said.

"You have lapses; sometimes you are almost rude, most abrupt, somewhat neglectful of your best friends."

"Oh, I say! That's not a very flattering picture. To which of my best friends have I been neglectful?" he asked.

"Myself—for one."

He looked surprised.

"That charge will not stand being put to the test," he answered.

"You have not been to see me since Ascot," she said.

"And that comes under the charge of neglect?"

"Yes. You consider me one of your friends?"

"Of course; don't ask foolish questions."

Alan looked particularly well this morning. He was a picture of health, a well-groomed man; his eyes were bright as he looked at her, thinking how lovely she was.

To Eve he was more attractive than ever. She loved him with her whole heart and soul, every nerve in her body thrilled toward him; and there he stood, smiling at her placidly, when she longed for him to take her in his arms, crush her, pour out a tale of love into her waiting, willing ears. Why could he not see it?

She held herself in bounds, but it was difficult.

"When do you join the Sherwoods?" she asked.

"I have joined; I am on leave. I have to put a lot of things straight at Trent Park. I had no idea there was so much to do."

"But you are not in uniform," she said.

"No; I thought I'd come over in ordinary attire—you might have been startled to see me in khaki."

"I certainly would have been."

"Eve, I want you to do something for me when I go away," he said.

Her heart beat fast, this was more promising.

"You know I am only too willing to do anything I can for you."

"That's good of you. I want you to keep an eye on things at Trent Park."

"You have a very capable housekeeper."

"Oh, yes; but even she wants supervising sometimes."

"And you think I can do it?" she asked with a smile.

"Nobody can do it so well; you are accustomed to manage, always have been. I've heard my father say so, and of course I've noticed it myself," said Alan.

He looked at her curiously, mischief in his eyes.

"I believe my governor was more than half in love with you, Eve," he said.

She felt hot, uncomfortable; Alan's father had been very much in love, or infatuated, with her.

"How foolish! Don't be absurd, Alan," she said hastily.

He had seen the change in her; he had sometimes wondered if

his father had paid attentions to her, then dismissed the idea as ridiculous.

"Is it absurd?" he asked.

"You must know it is," she said, with emphasis.

"The governor was rather a ladies' man," he said smiling. He saw she was uncomfortable, and teased her.

"He was very polite and considerate," she replied.

"More polite than his son, according to your version," he answered.

"I never said so."

"Not in so many words. You said I neglected my best friends."

"And it is true; you haven't been to see me for a month."

"I have explained why. I say, Eve——"

"Yes."

"Did you miss me? I mean did you want me to come and see you?"

"I did."

"You really missed me?" he asked again.

"Very much. Are you not my nearest neighbor? Have we not been old friends for many years? I do not like to lose old friends," she said.

"There is no danger of losing me. That will rest with yourself; I am always at your commands," he answered.

"Always?" she asked.

"Whenever you want me," he replied.

Want him! Did she not always want him? Why was he so blind?

"If there is war you will go on active service?" she said.

"I hope so; I don't want to remain here, kicking my heels in idleness," he replied with a laugh.

"No; I suppose that is natural. I shall miss you very much."

"It's nice to be missed. I'm a lucky fellow, Eve."

"Are you?"

"Yes; there's many a man would like to hear you say that—the Baron, for instance," he said.

She shrugged her shoulders.

"I think you are mistaken about the Baron," she said.

"He admires you, and didn't he give you the winner of the Derby?"

"But not the Hunt Cup," she replied with a laugh.

"No; but he wasn't far out," said Alan. "Then there's Harry Morby; he's your devoted slave."

"Is he? There's not much of the slave about him," she replied, smiling. "I suppose he's sorry you are not in your old regiment."

"He says so; I really believe he is."

"The Sherwoods are a famous cavalry regiment?" she asked.

"They bear an honored name, they have seen some service. I am lucky to get in there."

"You were always a good soldier."

"Glad you think so. There'll be no feather-bed soldiering this time."

"You seem positive there will be war?"

"Yes; absolutely certain."

"It will be a terrible thing."

"Awful; the slaughter will be great."

"And hundreds of thousands will lose their lives?"

"Yes; no doubt about that."

"I shall pray for your safety then, Alan."

"Don't get solemn about it—I'm not gone yet. You'll do as I ask? Just run over to Trent Park sometimes and let me know how things are going on. Sam Kerridge said I must tell you he'd always be very pleased to show you over the stud—good fellow, Sam. What else do you think he said?"

"I really can't guess."

"And I daren't tell you."

"Why not?"

"It's personal. Sam has a habit of blurting out what he thinks."

"Tell me what he said."

"He asked me a question when I spoke about your visiting the stud in my probable absence," said Alan.

"What was it?"

"'When's the wedding?'" he said.

Eve lowered her eyes.

"What a curious question," she said. "What did he mean, to whom did he refer?"

"Miss Eve Berkeley and my humble self," said Alan, laughing.

"How funny," she said.

"Yes; that's just what I thought. What the deuce put it into his head I don't know," said Alan, laughing.

"I suppose he thinks near neighbors sometimes marry," said Eve.

"Perhaps so. They do; I've noticed it. I say, Eve, wouldn't it be curious if we ended up that way?" said Alan.

"Ended up which way?"

"By marrying. How would you like it? Have you ever considered the prospect?"

"Have you?" she asked without looking at him.

"No, I can't say I have. I don't suppose you'd have me in any case."

"Oh! you don't think I'd have you! Well, consider it over—perhaps we might do worse."

"Eve, you're not serious! You haven't been looking at it from that point of view?" he said.

"I believe I'd marry you to-morrow if you asked me, Alan," she said smiling, in a half-joking tone, but her heart beat painfully fast.

"Good Lord, you don't say so!" exclaimed Alan, in such alarmed tones she could not help laughing.

"Please do not be alarmed," she said.

"Of course you're not serious! For the moment I flattered myself you were. You're joking. Funny, isn't it?"

"Supposing I am serious?" she said.

"By Jove, I believe I'd ask you! The temptation would be more than mortal man could resist," he said.

"Try! Let me see how you make love—I am sure you'd be eloquent."

"Don't let us carry this game too far, Eve; it might develop into something serious," said Alan.

"Something serious—good heavens, if he only knew!" she thought. "But what can a poor woman do with such a man. You are very blind, Alan."

CHAPTER XIV

INSIDE THE KEEP

Carl Meason was very busy. He sat up late, poring over maps, tracing routes. Abel Head said:

"He doesn't seem to have a minute to spare."

He had minutes to spare and they were devoted to paying attentions to Jane Thrush when he had an opportunity. She did not avoid him: he interested her, and her father appeared to like him.

Meason approached Thrush carefully, feeling his way gradually; he knew it would be best to influence the father in order to ingratiate the daughter.

Tom took him through the forest, pointing out places of interest. He found Meason a ready listener, who flattered him by remarking on the knowledge he possessed. They walked many miles, but Meason noticed he avoided going near the house in Trent Park. The moat aroused his curiosity. It was filled with water, the depth being considerable; a boat was moored to a small landing stage. Carl asked if his guide could take him into the keep.

Tom said:

"I have brought the keys with me; I thought perhaps you'd like to see it. I've seen strange sights hereabouts. I never come nigh the place at night: there's things chill the marrow in one's bones," and he gave a slight shudder.

Carl laughed. He was no believer in ghosts and such-like superstitions.

"Yer can laugh," said Tom irritably, "but I've seen 'em I tell ye. My eyes are good evidence, I can't doubt 'em."

"I was not laughing at what you thought you've seen," said Carl.

"Thought!" exclaimed Tom. "There's no thought about it; it's gospel truth."

"What did you see?"

"It's strange, beyond telling. There's been murder done in yon keep many a time; it's a gruesome place," and he pointed across the dark water to the round, ancient, tower-like building, whose stones gave evidence of many centuries' battling with storm and tempest.

"Looks a bit lonesome."

"It is. You see that spot near the wall? Well, it's dark and deep, and one night I saw her rise out from the depth. She wailed and threw up her arms, then she sank. She came up again, and a third time; then there was a splash and she disappeared. It was a great stone struck her down. From yon small window, that slit in the wall, I saw a face looking out. It was an awful face, must have been near kin to the devil's; the thing groaned, broke into a harsh laugh, and it vanished. Lord, I never want to see such sights again! My hair turned gray," said Tom.

Carl was amused. He humored him.

"Strange happenings indeed," he said. "What's it like inside?"

"I'll show you, but you had best go in alone. I've had enough of the d——d place," answered Tom.

He got into the boat, took the solitary oar and placed it in the rollock [Transcriber's note: rowlock?] at the stern; Carl stepped in and stood up.

"Best sit," said Tom; "it's a crazy old craft."

"Why doesn't Mr. Chesney have a new one?"

"Don't know; thinks it's good enough for the job, I expect. He never encourages folks' going to the keep."

"But he allows you to carry the keys?"

"Yes; he trusts me. He knows I'm none too fond of the devilish hole." Tom ferried across to the broken-down landing-place near the door of the keep. They got out.

"Here you are," said Tom. "Go inside if you wish."

Carl took the key.

"I'll not be long," he said, as he put it in the lock. It turned with difficulty, and as he pushed the nail-studded old oak door open there was a cool, damp, vault-like smell.

"Reckon you'll come out quick enough," said Tom. "Best be careful; there's some old broken steps lead down under the moat—a dungeon or summat's there." He swore as his foot slipped and he almost fell into the water.

"That's a sure sign we're not wanted here," said Tom gloomily.

Carl smiled and went inside. It was a curious, gruesome place, and the dank air was stifling. He climbed the stone steps upward until he came to a small room. The walls were bare but there were a bed and chairs and tables, all of oak, an iron ring in the wall, a rusty chain, and a padlock of huge size lay on the stone floor, unlocked. The slit in the wall gave enough light to see. Carl stood on a chair and looked out. He saw Tom, waved his hand, but there was no response.

"He can't see me," thought Carl. "It's strange; he's looking straight here."

There were more stairs. At the top he found another room exactly similar to the one below, furnished in the same bare way. In one corner he saw something gray. Examining it, it proved to be a flimsy gauze-like wrap; it was not old, nor torn. There was a white cloth, also a pair of soft slippers.

"The ghost's attire," thought Carl. "Somebody comes here and frightens people. Wonder what for? Probably to scare 'em away for some purpose of his, or her, own. This is interesting."

He replaced the garment, letting it fall and arranging it as nearly as possible as he found it. He went down again, feeling the wall as he descended. It was damp; drops stood out, burst and trickled down. He found the stone steps leading to the dungeon under the moat; they were smooth, broken in places. He was careful in stepping; a slip and he might be landed at the bottom with a sprained ankle, a broken leg, or worse. It was a slippery descent; once or twice he fell down; but he intended seeing what was at the bottom and at last succeeded.

The dark dungeon had a curious odor in it, probably due to the water and lack of fresh air; but there was a scent undefinable as well. He struck a match; it went out immediately, just as though somebody, or something, had blown upon it. He was not a nervous man, but when the second and third match went out in the same way he was inclined to beat a retreat.

"One more try," he thought, and struck three or four wax matches at once; this proved effective and gave him time to see in the corner, propped up, what looked like the body of a man. He must be mistaken; he lit more matches, dropping the others on the floor, where they spluttered in the wet and fizzled out.

It was a man, could be nothing else. He went toward the body, for such he supposed it, bent down to feel it, and found nothing. This was strange. He lit more matches. Now he saw space; there was no body there. He stepped back several paces, astonished, lost in wonder; then he saw the thing again, saw it distinctly, and it seemed to move. It came toward him, or in his excited state of mind he fancied so. His light went out; he had no more matches. As he groped his way to the steps, or where he thought they were, something touched him on the shoulder. It was enough to startle any man, and he cried out in alarm. There was a faint, squeaking noise and a fluttering, then the thing touched his cheek and he smelt a deathlike odor. Thoroughly alarmed he groped out. He felt the damp wall; he had lost the steps; he must walk round, feeling until he came to them, being a circular dungeon he must come to them. It seemed an interminable time before he came to the opening and began to scramble up on his hands and knees.

Tom Thrush waited in the boat. He thought him a long time gone and hoped nothing had happened. He knew it was a queer place to roam around. He whistled for company, then lit his pipe.

Why didn't he come out of the beastly place? What was that? It sounded like a startled cry; it came from the tower. Tom shivered. He wasn't going in there to look for Carl Meason, not for any money. The smoke came from his pipe in jerky whiffs.

Just as he was about to step out of the boat, go to the door and call, Carl Meason came out with a quick movement. Tom stared at him in amazement, not unmingled with fear.

Meason was covered in dirt and damp from head to foot, there was blood on his hands, his face was blanched, a wild look in his eyes. He had no time to pull himself together before Tom saw it. His recovery however was remarkably quick considering what he had gone through. He had no desire to give himself away. He looked at his clothes and laughed. In the open again his courage revived.

"It's the dirtiest damp hole I ever was in!" he said; and Tom recognized a difference in his voice.

"Yer all over filth," said Tom. "Yer hands are bloody, ye've torn yer trousers. Where've yer been? Have yer seen anything?"

"Rotten place," said Carl. "If I were Chesney I'd blow it up."

"Did yer see anything?" persisted Tom.

"What the deuce is there to see except bare walls and some ancient oak furniture, must be hundreds of years old."

"It is," said Tom, "more—hundreds and hundreds. You looked a bit scared when you came out—white as a sheet, eyes near shooting out of yer head. Tell me what yer saw."

"Nothing," said Carl. "The place gave me the horrors. I lost myself in the dungeon, took me a long time to find the steps again, that gave me a shock, I had no matches left."

"There's folks been put in that place never saw the light o' day again. Do you believe it's haunted?"

Carl made no reply for a few moments, then said:

"It may be; I shouldn't be surprised. I'm more inclined to believe you since I've been inside."

"I thought as how you would. Seeing's believing," said Tom.

"But I tell you I did not see anything. I heard sounds."

"Ah!" exclaimed Tom. "What like were they?"

"Groans!"

"It's them ye heard, the spirits of the dead; the poor devils never rest in peace," said Tom.

They were going across the moat. There was a splash and both started; Tom almost dropped the oar.

"What's that?" he said. "Look!" and he pointed to the ripples in the dark water circling.

"A fish rising," said Carl with a queer little laugh.

"There's no fish in here, don't believe there's even a carp in."

69

"Why not?"

"What 'ud fish be doing in this beastly hole?"

"Feeding."

"Nothing to feed on."

"You don't know what's at the bottom of that," said Carl, pointing downward.

"And I don't want to. If it's fish, I'd not eat them," said Tom.

They walked back to the keeper's cottage. Jane met them at the door, surprised to see the state of Carl's clothes. She asked where he had been.

"Exploring the moat and the keep," he replied, thinking her pretty face was a great help to banish phantoms.

Jane laughed as she said:

"You've had a fright. Keep away from the place, it's haunted; there's danger when you meddle with 'em."

"I saw nothing in the keep. I told your father so."

Jane shook her head as she replied:

"Best say nothing about it; keep those things to yourself."

"Have you ever seen things there?" asked Carl.

"Telling's knowing," said Jane, but without smiling.

CHAPTER XV

A SUDDEN PROPOSAL

War was declared against Germany on that fateful day in August; the blow had fallen at last, the nations of the earth were about to measure their millions, and England was unprepared. There was no doubt about the strength of feeling in Britain; every man was for war, with the exception of a few cranks and peacemongers, many of them little better than traitors to their country.

There was a call to arms; it echoed, reverberated, throughout the land; and never was such a voluntary response by any nation. There is little need to write about it; everybody knows how "Kitchener's chaps" rolled up in thousands, to their everlasting honor. By their response they showed the spirit of the nation, roused at last to a sense of horrible danger. Throughout the land there were martial sounds—the hum of camps, the tramp of men, the clang of horses' hoofs, the rattle of war department wagons. Before people had time to rub their eyes and become wide awake, an army had landed in France, eager to help gallant little Belgium, and stop the rush of the enemy's vast hordes.

The Sherwoods were mustered in Trent Park. A noble array they made, splendid men, well mounted and equipped, eager to get at the foe. Captain Alan Chesney was with them, his house the headquarters of the regiment. They had not to wait long; they were in luck's way, one of the first cavalry regiments ordered to the front.

Alan, busy preparing for his departure, had barely a minute to spare, but he made time to call on a few friends, and Eve Berkeley was one of the last. He rode to The Forest in uniform, looking every inch a soldier. He stood in the room waiting for her, his fingers drummed impatiently on the mantelpiece; he wanted to be away, the fighting spirit of the soldier was roused again when he put on khaki. He longed for war—and the front.

For some years he had been a peace soldier, spending money freely, having plenty of spare time, although he was never a laggard and loved the drill and discipline. Now it was different; they were off to the front, where the battle already raged furiously and danger threatened France, as in the former war and from the same source, with many times the strength.

Eve came in. She looked at her best. She knew he was coming and had been thinking of him. There was danger ahead for the man

71

she loved; it was possible she might not see him again. She dare not think of that, it was terrible.

He turned round quickly and came to her, taking both her hands. Looking into her eyes he could not fail to see the light in them; it dazzled but did not blind; it opened his to what was hidden behind the electric flashes in hers. For a few moments there was silence. Then he said:

"I am come to say goodbye, Eve, my old playmate, my best friend."

His voice was well under control, no tremor, but it vibrated and played on her heart-strings. She was agitated; she had been counting on this parting, thinking what might happen, re-changing many things.

"We leave to-morrow, or the next day. I go to London to-night. I cannot tell you our destination, but I can guess it."

Still she did not speak, and he went on:

"We shall give a good account of ourselves, the Sherwoods. Many of us will not return, but something tells me I shall come through it all and live."

"How I shall miss you!" she said. "It will be in fear and trembling I open the paper each morning and scan the lists. But you are doing right; no man can hang back at such a moment. You are glad to be in uniform again?"

"Indeed I am. I feel as though I had never been out of it," he answered.

"You look splendid," she said.

"This morning you are at your best," he replied.

"You were coming to see me, I wanted you to carry away a good impression," she said, smiling.

"I shall often think of you, Eve, and your many gracious actions. By Jove, you are a brick—there's nobody like you," he said enthusiastically.

She was pleased and showed it.

"Have you forgotten our last conversation?" he asked. "It was perilously near the danger zone."

"Why call it a danger zone?" she asked.

"Eve, you don't mean it?" he asked.

"Mean what?"

"Oh, you know. By Jove, I'll risk it, although I can't imagine such good fortune falling to my lot."

"What are you going to risk?" she asked, strangely agitated.

"Asking you to be my wife—there it's out—must I go?" he said.

"Do you wish to go?" she asked archly.

"No; there."

72

He almost lifted her off her feet as he took her to him and kissed her many times. She clung to him, her arms round his neck, her head resting on his breast; she seemed loath to let him go.

"Alan, oh Alan, it seems too good to be true! I thought you were never going to ask me. I am afraid I have schemed for this. Forgive me, I could not live without you," she said, and again he stopped her mouth with kisses.

"I have always loved you, Eve. When you were a girl you were different from anybody else, the only girl for me. You have not answered my question?" he said.

"I will be your wife, Alan; it has been the dearest wish of my life. I am almost afraid to say how much I love you," she said softly.

"Never be afraid of that; tell me, I want to carry it away with me."

She told him, and his body flamed in response, his heart beat fast. It was the most thrilling moment of his life; she buried her blushing face on his shoulder and panted for very joy.

Alan recognized the depth of her love and wondered at it. She was his, part of him. He felt it, henceforth they would be one. When he was away she would be with him in the spirit. He was loath to part from her, but it had to be. Duty called and that came first. He waited a few minutes until they were calmer.

"Marry me before I leave," he said impetuously.

"There is no time," was the faint reply. "You go to-morrow."

"I forgot; no, there is no time. It is not fair to ask you. Promise me if I come home for a day or two you will consent?"

"Readily, Alan. I am yours when you wish to take me," she answered.

"Supposing we do not leave to-morrow, supposing it is a few more days, that there is time?" he said, his eyes very bright and eager.

"If there is time——" she hesitated.

"You will?"

"Yes."

This was too much for him; he was overwhelmed at his happiness. He clasped her in his arms again and crushed her until it pained, but it was exquisite pain, she felt safe with those strong arms about her.

"I feel as though I never want to let you go again," he said.

She laughed happily.

"If there is time, Alan, we can be quietly married," she said.

"I shall try and make time. I must run no risks."

"Risks of what?"

"Losing you."

73

"That can never be now. You will not lose me. I may lose you," and she shivered.

"I'm not going to be killed, wounded perhaps. What if I come home minus an arm, or a leg, or with a mutilated face? You might wish to cry off our compact. I can't risk that, Eve; I want to make sure of you," he said earnestly.

"And do you for a moment suppose that would make any difference?" she asked.

"No, I don't, although I said as much. I have great faith in you."

They talked over the future for a long time. When he rose to go, he said:

"Remember, if there is time we are to be married before I leave for France."

"Yes; I hope there will be time," she said quietly.

"You would make a charming widow," he said jokingly.

"Don't say such horrible things," she replied.

"I won't offend again. There's too much in life to even hint at death," he said.

"Let me know if I can see you in London before you go to-morrow?" she said.

"I will; I'll send a special messenger."

"To my town house. I shall be there. I will go up to-night in order to be ready."

"You're the best of women!" he said, kissing her.

He was gone. She sent for her maid and gave orders about traveling to London in the afternoon. How happy she was! Alan had asked her to be his wife at last! She had waited a long time; it seemed almost too good to be true. She wished she could be married before he went away; then she would be quite sure of him. Now he was gone she wondered if her spell over him would ever be in danger of breaking. She blamed herself for such thoughts, but they would intrude, causing little pangs of uneasiness and doubt that irritated her.

On the journey to London she was filled with hope and fears. Their marriage would settle everything, give her the right to look after Trent Park and all belonging to it, of which she was capable, and knew it. There would be much to do in his absence; he had asked her before and she consented, but there were difficulties.

There were several stoppages on the way; inquiries elicited the information that traffic was congested owing to the movements of troops. Already war made a difference; what would it be in the course of a year?

Alan called late at night. There was no chance of a marriage, he was to leave in the morning. He fretted and fumed at the delay, but Eve dispelled his gloom and he went cheerfully after an affectionate parting. After his departure she sat in a disconsolate mood in the large room, longing for company. She wondered if she ought to make their engagement known. He had said nothing about it; perhaps better not until she heard from him. There was the satisfaction of knowing he loved her, that she was to be his wife. Even this did not dispel the shadows; she tried to convince herself all would be well—only partially succeeding.

As for Alan, in the rush and turmoil of departure he almost forgot the question of an immediate marriage. It could not take place yet, so why trouble about it? Eve was his and he was satisfied. On the whole he considered it perhaps as well they were not married. There was no telling what might happen to him and she would be in a better position if he succumbed to the chances of war. Not that he had any fears on that score; he looked forward to the coming struggle in a very optimistic mood.

CHAPTER XVI

JANE'S LOVE AFFAIR

The battle raged; the German hordes pushed forward; the great retreat began. Paris seemed about to fall and there was anxiety in the Allied forces. Prodigies of valor were chronicled in a few lines of space; the British army, greatly outnumbered, was holding the enemy. The advance was slow, a wonderful retreat, perhaps the most heroic known until almost equaled by the Russians later on.

Then came the news that the enemy was checked, they in turn were driven back when Paris seemed within their grasp. The Germans were held and the situation saved. It was marvelous, and the "little army," under Sir John French was covered in glory. Britain thrilled at the news of her soldiers' bravery. They fought as of old, fought as at Waterloo, at Inkerman, at the Alma, and Balaklava. They had not degenerated, the same spirit animated them; they knew how to die, and how to win. For forty years the Germans had been trained for war, and their masses were held up by men who had known peace for many years.

The Sherwoods had their chance and took it. The Uhlans were no match for them; they were bowled over like ninepins. Men and horses fell in heaps before the terrible charge. Captain Chesney was in the thick of it all. Rash, brave, knowing no danger, he was a typical cavalry officer; and that master of cavalry tactics, Sir John French, heard of his bravery and recognized it. After their first action Alan Chesney was the idol of the Sherwoods. The men followed him into the jaws of death and cheered as he led them on. Nothing could stand before them, their impetuosity overcame all obstacles; they lost many men but gained imperishable renown.

Eve Berkeley read the meager accounts of the fighting and grew impatient, longing for more, wondering why publicity was not given to the doings of the bravest of the brave. Alan's name cropped up once or twice, she gathered from the vague lines that he had done wonders, that his bravery was conspicuous, that his men loved him, and she was proud of him.

Week after week passed and she only had one or two lines from him. There was no time to write long letters, she must wait until he was out of the saddle for an hour or two. She knew how difficult it must be to write, yet longed to hear, and each morning looked for a letter. When it did not come she scanned the papers in fear and trembling. She little knew the narrow escapes he had already experienced, and he came out of terrible frays with hardly a scratch. When horses were shot under him a trooper was always ready with another for him with a "take mine, sir." Alan reveled in the fury of the charge; his whole body thrilled as he galloped down on the Uhlans at headlong speed. This was soldiering indeed; no playing; deadly, grim earnest, a toss-up for life or death. He grieved at the loss of men, but the fewer in number the more they were united and proved irresistible. During the retreat they were here and there and everywhere, scouting, thwarting the enemy, breaking up his plans, a thorn in his side pricking deep. Seldom out of the saddle, he had little time to think of home and Eve Berkeley.

At Trent Park things went on much as usual. Eve went over occasionally; her visits were in no way resented, everything was made smooth for her.

At the stud she was always welcome. Sam Kerridge appreciated her at her full worth; said she knew more about horses than half the men he met, that she had an eye for a good 'un, and could fault the inferior sort.

"Blest if I couldn't leave her in charge for a month without the slightest fear of anything going wrong," he said.

Alfonso had taken the place of Mameluke, and there seemed every chance of his being as popular with owners of mares, but the shadow of war over the land was likely to have some effect on the big studs. Already there was talk of cutting down expenses and selling off.

Carl Meason still had his rooms at the Sherwood Inn and Abel Head wondered if he were right in his surmise that he was a spy. He argued that a spy would hardly bury himself at Little Trent in war time; still, there was no telling. Meason went out in his motor at night more than usual; moreover he carried a very powerful light and there was an unusually strong one inside the car.

"What's this for?" asked Abel as he examined it.

"The police are very particular about lights, so I've got this ready in case one of the others goes out," was the reply.

"Must give a powerful glare," commented Abel.

"It does. Nothing like seeing far enough ahead," said Carl.

Abel was not satisfied. He had never seen such big lamps inside a car before and he did not believe Meason's reason for having it. Although he had plenty on hand Carl Meason found time to meet Jane Thrush. After much persuasion he induced her to go in his car to Nottingham to see the sights, and strange to say Tom raised no objections. Thrush seemed favorably impressed with Meason; no doubt an occasional fiver helped in this direction, for Tom was fond of money.

"Where's the harm?" he said to himself. "Jane's a clever girl, knows more than the ordinary, and she's good enough for any man. He seems sweet on her. No reason why he should not marry her. There's money, not a doubt or he couldn't sling fivers about like he does."

All the same he questioned Jane closely after her return from Nottingham; but she was reticent. Not given to talking much himself he did not pay so much notice to this as he might otherwise have done.

Carl Meason was a man to attract a girl like Jane Thrush. He could be agreeable when he chose; his face concealed his real feelings—it was a mask and effectually changed the man to outward appearances. Meason was making the mistake of his life. He was fast becoming infatuated with Jane Thrush, subordinating certain objects to her, spending time in her company. The work he had in hand brooked no interference. It was sufficiently dangerous; there must be no leakage. Not a hint or a whisper must get about or he would be in grave danger on both sides. His employers were ruthless, and the authorities in England would not be likely to spare even his life if they got wind of his purpose and how he was working.

Jane Thrush held him in the hollow of her hand did she but know it. At present she was too innocent to suspect his real nature and she never dreamed what he was about. She would not have understood his affairs had they been explained to her. Jane merely saw in him a well-to-do man, who talked to her with respect, and was evidently more than half in love with her. She was not conceited although she had a proper sense of her importance and good looks, which was fostered by her father.

During the drive to Nottingham and back Carl Meason made love to her in ardent fashion and she had not repulsed him although she was careful to keep him within bounds. One thing Tom Thrush had effectually taught his daughter and that was the perils to which pretty girls are exposed. He had made no bones about it, spoke out plainly, and Jane learned the lesson well.

"Her's got no mother," Tom said to himself, "and it's my place to warn her. She'd best know what's what and then she can't stumble with her eyes open," and in his rough way he saw farther than people who avoided responsibilities in this direction.

Jane was therefore well armed against the wiles of unprincipled men, although it had hitherto been her good fortune not to encounter any. There had been kisses and embraces and Jane accepted them without much enthusiasm or response. Carl Meason's lovemaking left her cold; somehow she hardly thought it

78

real. She did not tell Tom of these embraces and he forebore to push inquiries. His occupation made him suspicious and watchful; he was the terror of poachers and evil-doers among the game, and had tracked many notorious men down. Although he loved money he surmised that Carl Meason's occasional fivers were not given for nothing, they were to smooth the way for Jane's favor.

If the man meant well by his daughter there was no harm done; if ill, then he would settle with him in a way that would astonish before any damage was done.

Carl Meason quickly discovered he would have to play straight with Jane Thrush, also her father, and for once in a way he was inclined to do this; it was after all the easiest to get what he wanted.

So far he had never given much thought to taking a wife, but when he considered everything, turning the pros and cons over, he came to the conclusion Jane Thrush was worth some sort of sacrifice. He would not surrender any of his liberty, once she was his he would mold her to his will; he fancied this would be easy—he was mistaken, as better men have been.

It was a relief from his work to talk and make love to Jane, also to think about her at night when touring round the country in his motor. There were other things to think about, and sometimes he dreaded what might happen when the time came for the devilish engines of destruction to work. Carl valued human life little, except in the care of his own body, and had been instrumental in sending many to death. He knew there were thousands of Germans in the country; they had been spying out the land for years, and he wondered at the supineness of the authorities in allowing it. He cared little who won the war so long as he reaped his reward. He would have been willing to accept pay from both sides had it been feasible.

If he had a better side to his nature Jane Thrush seemed likely to find it, but even she would have to walk warily if in his power. Jane's pretty face had won a sort of victory over him; he acknowledged his submission with a wry grimace, thinking she would be called upon to submit in her turn.

Meanwhile Jane hesitated as to what she would do if he asked her to be his wife, as she believed he would. To solve her doubts, she asked her father. Tom eyed her curiously; he was sleepy and barely grasped her question.

"What did yer say, lass?" he asked.

"If Mr. Meason asks me to be his wife what answer shall I give him?"

Tom was awake now. This was important.

"He'll ask, you reckon?"

"I believe he will."

"Then please yourself, lass. He's a well-favored man, seems well off, he'd make a good husband," said Tom.

"Perhaps he would," said Jane doubtfully.

CHAPTER XVII

THE LAY OF THE LAND

Race meetings gradually dropped out, they were few and far between; there was more important business on hand.

Fred Skane had sole control of Alan Chesney's horses during his absence and picked up a race or two to meet expenses. Alan had given no instructions to sell any of his horses, but Fred used his judgment and let three or four go in selling races. Alan impressed upon him to prepare a couple of horses to match against Bernard Hallam's Rainstorm and Southerly Buster, for he was anxious to demonstrate the superiority of the English horses.

Mr. Hallam brought his trainer from Australia, and Jack Wrench—his name—was granted permission to train at Newmarket. It was not long before two sterling good horses, Catspaw and Bellringer, four and five years old respectively, were purchased to lead the Australians in their work. Both horses had won good handicaps and came into the market on the departure of their owner for the front. Mr. Hallam paid a stiff price for them, but Jack Wrench had been advised they were worth it. The Australian trainer was anxious to prove that Rainstorm and Southerly Buster were equal to the best handicap horses in England.

It soon got about in racing circles that there was likely to be a match between horses of Alan Chesney and those of Bernard Hallam. This news spread far and wide, and the Australians in the fighting line were as eager about it as anybody. The Anzacs had a terrible time in Gallipoli, and the Dardanelles generally, but they were always eager to discuss sport when the Turks gave them a rest for a few hours.

Time passed quickly, and already the death roll on both sides was terrible. Still Alan escaped unhurt, and Eve expected him home on short leave; his latest letter, however, gave no hope of this for some time, but he said he would make an effort later on when his horses were fit to run. He fixed up a match with Mr. Hallam for a thousand a side between The Duke and Southerly Buster, and Bandmaster and Rainstorm, the distances a mile and two miles. The Hunt Cup winner developed into a great stayer, and as he had a wonderful turn of speed he was sanguine of beating Rainstorm.

So many race meetings were abandoned that the Newmarket programs were extended to take their place in some measure, and the headquarters of the turf became very busy. Racing men were thankful for small mercies; the extra meetings were well attended and big fields turned out for the events.

Mr. Hallam was often at Newmarket, taking great interest in the work of his horses, and Wrench gave him encouraging accounts of their progress. Both horses came well out of their gallops with Catspaw and Bellringer, and the local touts were much impressed with them.

Rainstorm was voted a beauty; the Australian horse became popular and his portrait appeared in several papers, together with interviews with Bernard Hallam.

Ella Hallam spent much of her time at The Forest with Eve Berkeley and they were firm friends. Ella knew of Eve's engagement to Alan and heartily congratulated her. Whatever she might have thought about Alan's attentions to herself she never for a moment doubted his inclinations were toward Eve; being a loyal-hearted woman she accepted the situation.

Fred Skane came to Trent Park to see Sam Kerridge. They were cronies, had been for years.

"I suppose you'll win both matches," said Sam.

"Pretty sure of it. Bandmaster will beat Rainstorm anyhow whichever way the other goes," answered Fred.

"Queer Bandmaster should turn out a stayer," said Sam.

"He's bred to stay," replied Fred.

"But he's a Hunt Cup winner and I'd hardly have expected him to be up to two miles."

"Well he is—no mistake about it. I've tried him and I know," said the trainer.

"And you don't often make mistakes, Fred."

"I'm just as liable to be mistaken as other men, but when I've something to go upon I'm not far out," replied the trainer.

"Awful job, this war," growled Sam; "upsets everything. I've lost four of my best men, and some of the others want to join up."

"Can't wonder at it. We'll need every man we have to win outright."

"Suppose we shall," said Sam. "All the same it's hard lines on a chap when he's used to the men and they're used to him."

In the evening they walked to Little Trent and went into the Sherwood Inn for a chat with Abel Head, who gave them a cordial welcome. They were favorites, and he liked a talk about racing. While they were chatting, a motor horn was heard and Abel said:

"That's Meason coming back. He's earlier than usual."

The trainer and Sam had heard of Carl Meason and were aware of Abel's opinion about him.

"He's making a long stay with you," said Fred.

82

"I'm about tired of him, although I'll not deny he's a good customer and pays his way," said Abel.

Carl Meason looked into the snuggery as he was passing the door.

"Come in," said Sam. "You may as well join us."

Carl entered, took off his coat, and sat down.

"When's the great match to come off?" he asked. He was always posted up on racing; he liked a flutter and never lost an opportunity of getting a useful hint.

"Hardly know yet," said Fred. "I expect we'll have to wait until Mr. Chesney gets leave. He'll want to see both races run."

"And I suppose his horses will win both matches?" said Carl.

"I hope so," said the trainer.

"You're not certain?"

"One can never be sure where racing is concerned," said Fred.

Carl laughed.

"Then what about these big coups that come off? They're pretty sure about them."

"Of course there are real good things, but even they are bowled over," said Fred.

"Clever men, you trainers," said Carl.

"Some of them," said Sam, with a wink at Abel.

"No doubt about Mr. Skane's being one of the clever men," said Carl.

"Don't know so much about that; I've been done more than once," said Fred.

"Shouldn't have thought it," said Carl. "The man who did you must have got up very early in the morning."

"Going out to-night again?" asked Abel.

"Yes, walking; I have a little business on hand that concerns my happiness," said Carl.

"Sounds a bit like courting," said Sam.

"You're not far out," was Carl's reply. "I'm thinking of getting married," he added as he left the room.

"Who's the girl?" asked Sam.

"Can't say for certain. He's been thick with Jane Thrush for a long time; they go out together. She's been in his motor to Nottingham. Can't think what Tom's about to allow it."

"He'd be a good match for her, eh?" asked Fred.

"I'm none so sure about that. What do you say, Sam?" asked Abel.

"I don't know much about the man. Jane's a very pretty girl; she's quite good enough for him," said Sam.

"I wish I could fathom him," said Abel. "He's mysterious; them roads and maps is all a blind, I feel sure."

"What makes you think so?" asked Sam.

"Nothing in particular. He keeps on tracing and tracking, and marking out spots in red ink, but I can't make head or tail of 'em," said Abel.

"Leaves them about, does he?" asked the trainer.

"Sometimes."

"There can't be much harm in what he's doing," said Fred.

Abel shook his head doubtfully.

"If he hadn't been here before the war began I'd have him put down as a spy—I'm not quite sure he isn't."

"Spying what?" asked Sam.

"The lay of the land," replied Abel.

"What for? How will that help? You don't think the Germans will come inside England?" laughed Fred.

"Not by land. They may come overhead and do some damage. What about these Zepplins they've been building for a long time?" said Abel.

The trainer laughed; so did Sam Kerridge.

"You can laugh," said Abel, "but it's my belief they'll do some damage with 'em before long."

"And you imagine Meason is planning out routes for them—is that it?" asked the trainer.

"Something of the sort. Wouldn't put it past him," said Abel.

"I can't agree with you. If he were doing that he wouldn't leave his work about," said Sam.

"He leaves about what he likes. I'll bet he has some things he would not like to be seen," said Abel.

"It's a dangerous thing to be a spy," said Sam; "and I don't think he looks like one. He'd have no time for courting if he'd a job like that."

"For two pins I'd give information against him," said Abel. "If I get half a chance, and enough evidence to go on I'll do it."

"It is a serious charge to make," said Sam, and the trainer agreed.

As they walked home they continued the conversation, and Sam gave Fred to understand there was something suspicious about Carl Meason's movements.

"But it doesn't look much like spying. He's after Jane Thrush and means matrimony—he'd have no time on his hands for that," said Sam.

Carl Meason left the Inn and walked to the keeper's cottage. He saw him leave, gun under arm, and as he wanted the coast clear it suited his purpose. Jane opened the door when he tapped—she had come to know the sound.

"Father's gone out," she said.

"I saw him. I am glad; I want a few words with you alone," he replied. "I am going away for a time on business and I want you to go with me. I shall be lost without you."

"I cannot go away with you; you know that," she answered.

"Oh, yes, you can—as my wife?" he said. So he did wish to marry her. She was gratified. She had thought of late such was not his intention.

"You'll marry me?" she asked.

"That's what I've come for to-night, to ask you to be my wife."

She was silent. It was an important step to take. She liked him, but she was not sure she loved him, and she was a little afraid of him. She had caught glimpses of the brute in him once or twice; it revolted her.

"Where are you going?" she asked.

"To the sea. We can spend our honeymoon there."

"Where?"

"I cannot tell you until we are on the way. I want nobody round here to know my whereabouts," he said.

"And you wish me to go with you as your wife?"

"Yes."

"When do you start?"

"In a week or so."

"Then I will give you my answer in a day or two," she said quietly.

He remained late, trying to persuade her to say she would be his wife. He had to leave without being satisfied, and he was annoyed.

CHAPTER XVIII

TOM'S WEAKNESS

"Then he's come to the scratch! I thought he would. You're a clever lass, Jane," said her father.

"Nothing clever about it. I haven't given him much encouragement," she said.

"What are you going to do?"

"That's for you to decide."

"It concerns you more than me. Do you love him?"

"I'm not sure."

"Eh! Not sure—you've had time enough."

"He's difficult to understand," said Jane.

"In what way?" asked Tom.

"I can hardly say; it's hard to explain. He seems fond of me; he might make a good husband."

"What's amiss with him?"

"Oh, nothing; but sometimes he frightens me," she said.

"Good Lord, how?" exclaimed Tom.

"He's fierce at times—he's terribly determined even when he's making love."

"That proves he's in earnest."

"Perhaps so; it shows he wants me, anyhow."

"That's in his favor. He's offered marriage, so he means right by you."

"It's his only chance," she replied.

Tom thought there was a good deal of common-sense in her; he put it down to his credit that he had brought her up well, opened her eyes.

"He must have money. Perhaps I'd better have a talk with him."

"What about?"

"He ought to settle a sum on you," said Tom cautiously.

Jane smiled as she thought: "You want money out of him, but you mean well."

"Men with cash generally give their wives a bit down," said Tom.

"If he did that, wouldn't it be rather like buying me?" she asked.

"Lord, no! Rich folk do it, the swells. Why shouldn't he?"

"He's not what I'd call a swell—real gentleman—not like Mr. Chesney," said Jane.

"That's different; there's not many men like him."

"No, that's true," said Jane with a sigh.

"I'll put a few questions to him," said Tom. "Wonder what his business is?"

"Surveyor; he says so."

"Can't make it out why he hangs about here so long without it's for your sake, lass."

"Perhaps that has something to do with it."

"Must have," said Tom.

He waited to see Carl Meason, who came the next morning, eager to have Jane's answer. He had a long talk with Tom Thrush; they went for a walk; Carl returned alone. He at once put the question to Jane, saying he had her father's consent. She made up her mind quickly. It was a chance she must not let slip—there were no eligible suitors in the neighborhood.

"I will marry you, Carl," she said. "You must be very good and kind to me."

He drew her to him, and kissed her passionately, vowing he would do everything possible to make her happy. He would have promised anything to gain his own ends.

"I want to be married in Little Trent Church," she said.

"I'll get a special license," he replied. "We've no time to wait."

"You're in a hurry to be off," said Jane.

"Business, my dear. I'd not have stayed so long at the Sherwood Inn if it hadn't been for you."

"You do love me—it's not make-believe?"

"Is that make-believe," he said, crushing her in his arms, kissing her many times. She recognized it was anything but make-believe; he wanted her badly, he must love her.

"Let me go," she said, panting.

"You believe me?"

"Yes, I believe you."

"And you love me?"

"Yes."

He crushed her again, then reluctantly let her go and stood looking at her.

"I've seen the parson," he said. "He's a queer old fellow; said he must see your father about it—and you."

"That's quite right. We sort of belong to him; he's our guide. I go to church."

"I told him he'd have no difficulty with you, or your father, that you'd both consent," he said.

87

"But you didn't know we would!" she remonstrated.

"I was sure of it," said Carl.

When he left, Jane wondered if he had promised or given her father any money; she half suspected there had been some bargaining and resented the thought. She knew her father loved her dearly, but he also loved money and would go far to get it.

Tom Thrush came home, putting a bold face on, but looked rather sheepish.

"It's settled; I've taken him. We're to be married in Little Trent Church. Parson's coming to see us about it," she said.

"Drat him, what's he coming for?" said Tom irritably.

"Carl says we're to be married as soon as possible by special license. I suppose that's what he's coming about," replied Jane.

"He's in a hurry."

"We're going to the sea—for the honeymoon," said Jane, blushing prettily.

"She's a beauty," thought Tom. "I wonder if she could have done better for herself?" He was seldom satisfied with anything.

"Where to, what seaside?" he asked.

"He said he could not tell me before we left. He didn't want the people about here to know."

"That's queer. Why shouldn't he?" growled Tom.

"He's good reasons for it, no doubt," she answered. "Was anything said about money?"

Tom shuffled uneasily in his chair.

"Well, yes, we had a few words about it."

"What did you say to him?"

"Told him it was usual for a man of means to settle something on his wife."

"Well, what did he say?"

"Laughed; said he wasn't exactly a rich man but he could afford to keep a wife in comfort. Then he offered to give me a hundred pounds to put by for you in case anything happened to him. He said it would do for a bit until his affairs were settled. I said it wasn't much. We argued the thing out. He's promised two hundred; that's not so bad," said Tom in a hesitating way.

"Did he give you the money?" she asked,

"No, he's bringing it to-night."

"To hand it to me?" she asked.

"I said I'd best keep it for you until you wanted it."

Jane smiled.

"You'll be sure and take care of it, Dad?" she said.

"Upon my soul I will. You know I'm a careful man with money, Jane," he said eagerly.

"I shall want a little pocket money when I go away."

"He'll give you some. He's sure to be generous."

"I think he has been generous in giving you two hundred pounds. I shall not ask him for any. You can spare some," said Jane.

"Of course it's not mine; it's yours," protested Tom. "But where's the harm in getting a bit more? He knows we're not well off."

She shook her head.

"No," she said. "I will not ask him, and you must not."

"Very well, my lass. Suppose we say ten pounds."

"Not enough; it must be twenty at the least."

Tom gave in at once. She might refuse to let him hold the money for her; that would be a calamity. Jane regarded this transaction with Carl Meason doubtfully. It was too much like bargaining for her; but she loved her father, knew his weakness, and forgave. After all, the money was hers, and he was honest and would not touch a penny of it; he merely wanted to gloat over its possession.

Carl Meason saw Tom Thrush alone and handed over the two hundred pounds. He was generally free with his money, and well supplied.

"Jane'll have to go to Nottingham to buy a few things before she's married," said Tom, feeling his way. He had promised Jane not to make more demands on Carl, but this did not include broad hints.

"I'll take her over," said Carl.

"That's all right; I can't afford to give her much," said Tom.

Carl grinned, rather savagely, inwardly cursing Tom for a greedy, miserly man. Well, he'd have Jane—that was his reward.

"I'll see to it my wife shall have all she wants," he answered.

"You'll not find her extravagant; she's been well brought up," said Tom.

"Trust her father for that," said Carl.

Jane went to Nottingham with Carl Meason; she found him liberal. He bought her expensive dresses and wraps; she began to have a sense of importance.

Tom Thrush was surprised. Jane had never seemed quite so good-looking; he considered Carl Meason had secured a valuable prize.

"I'll not deny he's dealt liberally with you," said Tom; "but you're worth it."

Carl Meason was satisfied when he saw Jane dressed at her best. She was even prettier than he thought; her new clothes certainly brought out her good points to perfection. The scruples of the parson were overcome after he had talked freely with Tom and Jane. He had doubts about the wisdom of the match, but kept them to himself.

They were married in Little Trent Church and Eve Berkeley was present. She had been much surprised when Jane told her she was to be married to Carl Meason.

"Are you quite sure you love him, Jane?" asked Eve.

Jane was not quite sure, and said so. Eve warned her she was about to try a dangerous experiment, run considerable risk.

"I am very fond of you, Jane, and I want to see you happy," she said. "Consider it well; there is time to draw back. You do not know much about Mr. Meason—nobody does; he is rather mysterious."

After this interview with Eve Berkeley, Jane had doubts as to the wisdom of the course she was pursuing; they vanished when out of her presence.

There were several villagers in the church and Jane's appearance created a mild sensation. She seemed quite the lady, exceedingly pretty. They had hitherto considered her as one of themselves, now she looked superior.

Carl Meason was proud of his young bride, but he wanted her all to himself, and after a brief stay of a couple of hours they left the Sherwood Inn in his motor and started on their journey amidst the cheers of the villagers. Carl had taken care to leave a liberal amount of money with Abel Head for the villagers' benefit; he wished to create a good impression and succeeded—for a time.

Tom Thrush made the most of his hours at Sherwood Inn. He was a temperate man, but this was a special occasion. There was an ample supply of liquor, to which he did full justice. The thought of returning to his cottage and finding no Jane there made him feel lonely and he remained at the Inn until closing-time.

Abel Head walked some of the way with him, and as they were about to part, said:

"I hope Jane will be happy. She's a good girl, far too good for Meason I'm thinking."

"Her'll be all right," said Tom. "The man's behaved well; he'll be proud of her, you see if he's not."

CHAPTER XIX

HALF A HEAD

The matches were to take place at Newmarket on the first two days. They had been arranged so that Alan Chesney might be present; leave was granted for five days, and he hurried home from the front. Since the desperate cavalry fighting with the Uhlans he had been promoted to the general staff in a special capacity kept a profound secret to all except those immediately concerned, and had already done excellent service.

He arrived at Trent Park late in the evening, and at once went to The Forest where Eve Berkeley anxiously awaited him. Bernard Hallam and Ella were there but discreetly kept out of the way until they met. Alan was bronzed and looked fit; Eve was proud of him. They had much to talk over, and for an hour were left to themselves. No mention was made of their marriage; it was understood it was to take place as soon as possible.

When Bernard Hallam and Alan were alone the matches between their horses were the subject of conversation.

"You've not seen 'em," said Bernard, alluding to Rainstorm and Southerly Buster. "You'll be a bit surprised. I shall give you a good run; it will probably result in winning one each."

Alan smiled; he had frequently heard from his trainer and was confident of success.

"Skane tells me your horses are better than he expected, but he thinks I shall win," he said.

"And my man Wrench says I shall," was the reply.

"There's a lot of interest in them, and the wagering will be close," said Alan.

"The odds will probably be on your horses; that's only natural. Would you care to have a wager as well as the stake?"

"I'm agreeable if you wish," said Alan.

"Then suppose we say an even five hundred on each race?" said Hallam.

"That will suit me," was Alan's reply.

Ella greeted Alan without any embarrassment. She had at first been touched by his attention to her, but directly she was certain he and Eve were in love she relinquished any hopes she might have had. Alan did not conceal his pleasure at meeting her, and Eve felt a slight touch of jealousy which she quickly banished as a foolish fancy. They were good friends, why should she not be pleased it was so?

They went to Newmarket by motor early in the morning and drove direct to the course. Alan was anxious to see the four horses; they were in the paddock, although The Duke and Southerly Buster were only due to run the mile that day.

The Australians attracted a crowd and pleased the public; they were a good-looking pair, Rainstorm being the favorite.

Alan was much impressed. He recognized his horses would have to be at their best to beat them; this Fred Skane assured him was the case. He went to look at The Duke and Bandmaster, and his hopes of winning rose. They were in splendid trim; the trainer had taken a lot of trouble with them. Eve was naturally anxious for Alan to win. Ella was quite convinced her father's horses would put up a good race; she had a couple of small wagers on with her friends.

Mr. Hallam found no difficulty in getting odds of six to four against Southerly Buster in the ring; the bookmakers were disposed to field against the Australian representatives. The match was regarded as an important event and placed third on the card. When the horses came out there was much cheering. It was a sporting affair in every sense of the word. There were plenty of Australians in khaki, eager to show their faith in Southerly Buster. Many of them were wounded, some known to Bernard Hallam and Ella.

The course was the straight mile, and there is no better galloping ground. Southerly Buster cantered down with Bradley in the saddle; the Baron's jockey fancied his mount, he had ridden him in several gallops. Tommy Colley was, as usual, on Alan's horse. It seemed an equal match both as regards the riders and horses. Naturally there was prejudice in favor of The Duke, odds of five to four being laid on him, then six to four was freely laid.

"Going to beat you, Ben," said Tommy at the post.

"You may, but you'll not find it easy; mine's a real good horse," was the reply.

They sprang off together, at top speed in a few strides, and it was evident the mile would be covered in fast time. Southerly Buster was a clinker over the distance, holding the Australian record for a mile, a generous horse, always willing to do his best. The Duke had a temper, but Colley knew his peculiarities and humored him. The horse had a bad habit; getting off well, he generally slackened speed after going a couple of furlongs. He did so on this occasion and Southerly Buster gained a length or more, much to the consternation of backers of Alan's horse. At the end of four furlongs the Australian had increased his lead and still The Duke held back.

Colley was anxious. The Duke had a tremendous turn of speed, but nearly three lengths was a lot to make up in half a mile.

The black, orange hoops and cap were conspicuous; Bernard Hallam fancied they would be as successful here as in Australia.

Jack Wrench had a habit of giving a long and prolonged whoop when he felt sure of a horse's victory. He proclaimed his confidence in Southerly Buster in a manner causing people near to laugh heartily. Hallam heard the well-known cry and it increased his hopes of winning.

Alan was disappointed so far at The Duke's form. He knew Colley was not quite as good as Bradley in a match, although his judgment was excellent, hardly ever at fault.

They were two furlongs from the winning-post and Tommy wondered when The Duke would put on full pressure; it was high time if he were to win. He dare not hit him, not at present; a few strides from the post it was generally effective because The Duke had no time to think things over and sulk. Just as Colley was beginning to despair and becoming desperate he felt The Duke bound under him, and in a few seconds the whole aspect of the race changed. So sudden was the move that Alan gasped. Eve clutched his arm in her excitement.

"By Jove, he's coming and no mistake!" exclaimed Alan.

"Splendid!" said Eve. "What wonderful speed—but will he catch him?"

"Whoop, whoop, whoop!" came from Jack Wrench—three sharp, piercing cries; but there seemed to be a note of alarm in the last, it died away suddenly.

The Duke was now almost at Southerly Buster's quarters, and Bradley was on the lookout for squalls; the advantage he possessed was greatly in his favor at this critical point. Colley thrilled with excitement; after the first part of the race the change was delightful. There was no doubt about The Duke's doing his best now. A tremendous cheer came from the crowd as he drew almost level with Southerly Buster.

They were not many lengths from the winning-post; it was a terrific set-to. There was nothing between the pair; they were evenly matched. The Australian was a wonderful horse. How the colonials cheered! There was nothing wrong with their lungs, whatever there might be with their limbs. It was a glorious sight to watch these two horses, representatives of all that was best in the sport on two sides of the world, struggling for supremacy. There was the blue blood of the English thoroughbred in both, although reared and trained under different conditions. Cheering and counter-cheering echoed over the heath as The Duke and Southerly Buster struggled on.

Whichever won, the honors were almost equal; this is as it ought to be on a match of this kind.

The whips were out; down they came, and still the horses were locked together. The Duke tossed his head. Colley thought it was all up, that he had given in; then to his surprise the horse's resentment took another turn and he made a savage effort to get his head in front.

The din was tremendous, and the excitement great; there was not likely to be a better race than this in the four days.

Bradley rode splendidly, so did Colley, and both horses put in all they knew.

They were just at the post when The Duke made his final stride. Had he won? Nobody knew, not even the jockeys; each thought he had just got it. The judge was certain; he alone could decide, and he did not hesitate.

There was a moment of silent suspense, then the hurricane of cheers as number one, The Duke's number, went up. Alan's horse had won by half a head in the last stride and Southerly Buster was only just vanquished. "Honor's divided," was Mr. Hallam's comment when he met Alan in the paddock.

"They are," he replied; "there is nothing between them."

"Only half a head," answered Mr. Hallam, smiling, "but it makes all the difference."

"I thought I'd just done it," said Bradley.

"So did I," said Colley. "It was the last stride; they were dead level next moment."

"It was worth coming home for," said Alan enthusiastically. "There'll be some fun at the front to-night. There were several wagers on. They are all great sports."

"Will they hear the result?" asked Eve.

"Oh, yes; you've no idea how news gets round; it's remarkable where it comes from—Lord only knows," said Alan.

There was much speculation in Newmarket during the evening as to the next day's match. Southerly Buster had run such a race that it was considered Rainstorm, who was the better horse, had a splendid chance of beating Bandmaster. Many people doubted the Hunt Cup winner's capability to stay two miles. Mr. Hallam was so impressed with Southerly Buster's performance that he laid several big wagers Rainstorm would win. Alan was not oversanguine, although Fred Skane declared Bandmaster's task was easier than The Duke's.

Baron Childs invited Alan, Evelyn Berkeley, and the Hallams to stay with him for the night; he also had other friends there.

During the evening there was some wagering on the next day's match and opinions were about equally divided.

The Baron was particularly attentive to Eve. Alan smiled as he said to himself:

"He does not know we are engaged. Eve is mine; there's no chance for anybody else."

Alan walked to Skane's after dinner and had a long talk with him over the running of his horses.

"Think we'd better put Robin Hood over the sticks," he said. "I've found out he's a good fencer; there'll be some meetings under National Hunt rules during the winter and next spring."

Alan was pleased at the suggestion; he loved a ride over the sticks or steeple-chase course, and Robin Hood was just the mount for him.

CHAPTER XX

TWO STAYERS

When Rainstorm and Bandmaster cantered down the course they were greeted with cheers; the second match was regarded with even more interest than the first.

The element of doubt about the staying powers of Bandmaster caused odds to be laid on the Australian, who had the reputation of a long distance winner. Alan was rather surprised at this, and supported his horse freely in order to make him favorite. This he did not succeed in, as the colonials laid short odds freely on Rainstorm.

Both horses were fit; they went moving past in free and easy style. Some said Bandmaster was a bit above himself; another gallop or two would have made all the difference, but the trainer said no; the horse always did better when a trifle big.

They were to run over the last two miles of the Caesarewitch course, a sure test of a horse's stamina.

They were sent on their journey at once and Rainstorm made the running. Wrench told Bradley he need not fear making as much use of him as he thought fit.

Colley was content to wait, keeping well in the track of the leader. Skane said to him before he mounted:

"Don't bustle him, let the other fellow make the pace; come as fast as you like at the end of the first mile, he'll think it's another Hunt Cup gallop. He's got the speed, we all know that, and I want to prove he's a stayer as well."

Rainstorm reveled in the going, which was fairly hard. He loved to hear his feet rattle; this was the sort of ground he was used to. Bandmaster seemed indifferent to the going, he galloped just as well when the ground was heavy; his temper was of the best, an easy horse to ride, always ready to run a genuine race.

Colley knew he was going well, and was content to wait for the end of the first mile as Skane had told him.

There was much jubilation as Rainstorm came striding along in front; this time no doubt the result would be in favor of the Australian. Mr. Hallam was satisfied; his favorite was going in his best form; the honor of Australia would be upheld, he felt certain of winning.

Fred Skane looked on with a smile of satisfaction. At the end of the first mile Bandmaster was going as strong as when he had started, and had not been at full speed. He waited for Colley to bring him along, thinking there would be a surprise for the folks who regarded the horse as a non-stayer.

Alan, despite the trainer's assurance, still had doubts about his horse. He thought Bandmaster was running unkindly, and put it down to his objections to going the distance.

Colley still waited, and Fred Skane wondered if he had mistaken the distance. The jockey had not, but it occurred to him Bandmaster's run would come better at the six furlongs than the mile. Skane gave him discretionary powers because he knew the horse and how to ride him.

"Here he comes," said Skane to himself, as he fixed his glasses on the horse.

Bandmaster responded to Colley's call; he dashed forward at a great pace and drew almost level with Rainstorm. This was a revelation to doubters, and some wagers were laid that Alan's horse would win.

Bradley, having been just beaten on Southerly Buster, was determined to turn the tables this time. Jack Wrench told him what a great horse Rainstorm was, one of the best stayers in Australia. "Nearly as good as Carbine," he said.

This, combined with his own opinion that Bandmaster was only a miler, made him sanguine, and when Rainstorm made the running without an effort he considered the race at the end of ten furlongs as good as won.

It came as a surprise when Bandmaster drew alongside, but he considered this effort a flash in the pan, anticipating the horse's falling back. At the end of another furlong Bandmaster still stuck to his work, and Colley appeared to be taking things easily.

"He's trying to fox me," thought Bradley.

Four furlongs from home Alan's horse was still going strong, showing no signs of shirking or giving way under pressure.

Bradley began to have doubts. Bandmaster traveled like a stayer, no doubt about it; still he could not quite believe he would last it out.

Rainstorm lacked one thing, a fine turn of speed to finish up with; this was where Bandmaster came in.

Colley urged his mount forward and headed his opponent. Bandmaster showed in front, and Bradley began to niggle at Rainstorm in order to keep his place. The Hunt Cup winner was traveling almost as fast as at Ascot and so great was the pace that Rainstorm felt the pressure. There seemed every possibility of this race's being as close as the first; it was astonishing how well the horses were matched. If anybody had doubts about the merits of Australian horses they were being rapidly dispelled.

There was a bigger crowd than the previous day, for the great race between The Duke and Southerly Buster roused sporting enthusiasm to a high pitch. The best patrons of racing were present, men who thoroughly enjoyed a match of this kind and were content with a fiver on the one they fancied.

The cheering began when the pair reached the stands, and was renewed again and again.

Alan was keenly interested in the result. If Bandmaster beat Rainstorm he would be delightfully surprised. He smiled as he pictured Fred Skane crowing over the doubters and pronouncing Bandmaster the best horse in the land.

Eve was anxious. She wanted Alan to win both matches; at the same time she was glad Mr. Hallam's horses showed such good form. She was quite willing to accept his excuse that they would have done better had they been thoroughly acclimatized. There was, however, little time to think over these things; all attention was concentrated on the race, which was now at the most exciting part, and the tumult at its height. The brown jacket with the blue sleeves held the lead as they came up the rise, but the black and orange hoops were close on to them, and Rainstorm's head was at Bandmaster's girth.

It was a punishing finish, but neither horse gave way—a splendid display of dogged courage and endurance, it appealed to all that was best in thousands of people witnessing it.

Bradley roused himself for a final effort; few jockeys had his strength at the end of a severe course; he had snatched races out of the fire by sheer power of endurance.

Tommy had beaten him yesterday; he was almost savagely determined not to be placed second to-day. Every nerve was strained, all his resources, and they were many, were called upon. He rode with his head as well as his legs, and judged every little thing in favor of his mount.

If Rainstorm had a bit of brilliant dash in him all would be well, but had he? From the way the horse had traveled Ben doubted but nevertheless determined to test him to the utmost. He felt the horse roll a trifle and held him firm. What caused this? He was certain Rainstorm was not beaten.

Then Bandmaster did the same thing, but it was more of a lurch and Colley gasped in surprise. Both jockeys were straining to the utmost but had not drawn their whips. Bradley was the first to raise his arm; Colley saw it and immediately followed suit. The whips came down simultaneously, the result was equal and the horses kept their positions. Again the whips fell and this time it was Bandmaster made the better response.

It was not a cruel race; these reminders were not vicious, so sensitive were the wonderfully bred horses that they answered to the least call.

Alan's horse gained half a length and there was a terrific cheer; the brown and blue was well in front, the black and orange hoops fell back.

A look of disappointment stole over Bernard Hallam's face. Rainstorm was his favorite; he would have given much to see him win. Two miles was his best distance. What a horse Bandmaster must be to beat him! A Hunt Cup winner giving Rainstorm the go-by over two miles—it was hardly credible; but there was the hard fact.

"Ah!"

Mr. Hallam exclaimed loudly.

"Hurrah!"

He shouted at the top of his voice.

"Hurrah, hurrah, hurrah!"

The cry came again in three loud, victorious cheers.

And what caused it? Why this sudden change from despondency to joyful hope of victory?

Rainstorm, after a prodigious effort on Bradley's part, drew level with Bandmaster, got his head in front, kept it there, and the judge's box was only a few yards away. A wonderful bit of riding, a great and gallant effort on the part of a good horse.

Tommy almost yelled as he drove Bandmaster along; to be defeated after all, no, he couldn't stand that. He never rode a better race and he had a good horse under him.

The last effort made by Rainstorm seemed likely to carry him first past the post, and Bernard Hallam was sure of winning. Bandmaster, however, would not be denied, the horse divined there was danger of losing; being full of courage he resented this and put forth his strength and speed to stave off defeat. How he did it Colley could not tell, but by some almost magical power he drew level with Rainstorm again and the desperate struggle continued.

The best thoroughbred never knows when he is beaten; so it was in the case of Bandmaster, who hung on to his opponent with bulldog tenacity. Bernard Hallam hardly believed it possible that Alan's horse had again got on terms with Rainstorm. The angle was deceiving and his colors still appeared to be in front; so thought hundreds of others.

For a brief moment the eyes of the jockeys met; each saw grim determination there, then they looked ahead and the judge's box loomed up clear and close.

The finish was thrilling. As they flashed past the post the question was asked, "What's won?" and nobody could tell.

"Close as The Duke's race," said one.

"Gone one better; Rainstorm won," said one of the Australians.

"Don't think so; that was a terrific run of Bandmaster's," replied another.

The numbers seemed a long time going up, then number one was slipped in; before the roar of Bandmaster's supporters died away number two appeared alongside it. The result was a dead heat—a mighty struggle—a dead heat over two miles. The owners were not likely to run it off, so which was the better horse was not settled and there would be much food for argument.

CHAPTER XXI

THE RAID

"We shall have to make another match to settle the question," said Mr.

Hallam.

"I'm willing," laughed Alan, "but give me time. I must go back at once; there's some tough work to be done before long."

"When you like," replied Mr. Hallam. "I am not going back to Australia at present. I have no wish to be sent to the bottom of the sea."

Alan said good-bye to Eve at The Forest. Before leaving for London he saw Duncan Fraser. Everything was going well, no cause for anxiety, and the manager spoke hopefully of the future.

Alan was surprised when he heard of Jane Thrush's marriage and rated Tom soundly for "throwing her away" on such a fellow.

Tom remonstrated in a sullen way, saying he thought it a good match for his daughter.

"You'll find out it is not," said Alan sharply. "The man is probably in the pay of the enemy, and will be laid by the heels before long; then she will come back to you and you'll be glad to have her."

Alan suspected Tom had been bribed by Meason; he knew his fondness for money but did not question him on this subject.

Tom Thrush thought over what Alan said. It caused him some uneasiness. He had a great respect for him and his opinions and knew he would not make an assertion without good grounds for doing so.

Carl Meason and his wife arrived at a small resort on the East Coast and stayed at an hotel. She wondered why he came here; there was not much to see, it was dull. Once she had been to Scarboro' and enjoyed the brief stay, but H—— was a different place.

Meason left her alone a good deal. The excuse was he had work to do; he did not explain what it was.

After a week in Meason's company Jane already began to repent her hurried marriage. Carl was rough; some of the veneer wore off rapidly. He gave her money and told her to amuse herself, but there was little chance of that in such a place.

"Why don't you take me with you? I'd like to see the country," said Jane.

"Can't be done, my dear; not yet, at least. Wait a week or two and I may be able to do so," he replied.

"What are you so very busy about?" she asked.

He declined to gratify her curiosity and said a wife ought to trust her husband; to which she responded that he didn't seem to trust her.

"Perhaps you'd rather go back to your father?" he sneered.

"You are unkind; you know I would not, but I think you might be with me more; it's lonely here," she said with tears in her eyes.

He kissed her, talked soothingly, and she was pacified. When alone she wondered what he was about. She thought the proprietor of the hotel and others regarded him with suspicion; it made her uneasy; she began to consider what Abel Head and others had said about him at Little Trent.

Already Zeppelin raids had been made on the coast, also S.E. counties, but Jane paid little heed to them. She looked at the pictures but they gave little information.

Carl came back very late, or rather early in the morning; she had gone to bed in a depressed state. What kept him out until this hour? It was three o'clock when he came into the room. She sat up in bed, the light was burning, and looked at him half frightened.

"I thought you were never coming," she said. "Where have you been?"

He locked the door, then sank into a chair exhausted.

"I'm tired out," he said.

"Where have you been?" she asked again.

"I went to ——; the car broke down; I had to have it repaired. It's all right now; I'll take you out to-morrow, Jane," he said.

This pacified her, but as she looked at him she fancied she detected signs of fear in his face; there was a furtive, hunted look about him. There was startling news in the papers next morning. A Zeppelin raid on the Norfolk coast was reported. Several people were killed and injured.

There was much excitement in the hotel; nothing else was talked about, and Carl Meason was regarded with curiosity. It was known he had been out in his motor until the early hours of the morning—perhaps he had seen the Zeppelins.

Questions were put to him. He replied that he saw nothing of them; his car broke down and it was a long time before he got it repaired. He was miles away in a lonely part of the country when it happened; fortunately he knew all about cars and the works; it was a great advantage to put your car right when it went wrong. He spoke freely, courting questions, made comments on the raid. He

102

had recovered his self-possession during the few hours' rest and was willing to meet all comers.

Jane was packing in her room when he went downstairs; he told her they would leave in the afternoon. After all it was a dull place for her and another part of the country would suit her best, or would she prefer to go to London for a few days?

She said she would love to see London, she had never been there; it must be a grand place.

He promised to consider it over and left her in the room.

Carl went out to examine his car; he was very particular about it.

"Nobody's been meddling," he thought; "it's just as I brought it in. It was a deuce of a run, exciting while it lasted. I don't think anybody spotted me."

When Jane reached the foot of the stairs she heard people talking in the private bar. There were three or four of them, she concluded, but the door was almost closed and she could not see inside. One voice she recognized as the landlord's.

The mention of her husband's name caused her to stand still and listen. The men were discussing the raid, from which she gathered that it was supposed the Zeppelins were guided by a motor car with a powerful light. Strong remarks were passed and hopes expressed that the scoundrel would be caught. It was surmised he was in the pay of the Huns—a spy—and he deserved shooting.

"He's a mysterious fellow," said the landlord, alluding to Carl Meason. "He was out in his motor half the night, came home between two and three. I'd like to know where he went; if I had something definite to go on I'd give warning to the police."

"You'd better do that in any case," said one of the men. "You'll be on the safe side then."

"That's all right," said the landlord, "but I might get into trouble if there's nothing wrong with him."

"Risk it, Frank; it's worth it. There's no end of these spies about, and the sooner they're stopped the better."

"I'll think it over—if he's a spy I'm sorry for his wife. She's a pretty quiet little woman, far too good for him."

Jane heard this conversation; she saw the door move and stepped into the hall. It was the landlord looked out and wished her good-day.

"I have been packing," she said, with a faint attempt at a smile.

"You are leaving?" he asked.

"I believe so. My husband talks about going this afternoon," she replied.

103

"He has not said anything to me at present. He's outside looking over his motor; he had a breakdown yesterday—lucky he could put it right. He was a long way from a town—Norwich would probably be the nearest," said Frank Spatts, the landlord.

Jane looked at him inquiringly. Carl told her he had the car repaired at ——. This was another tale.

"Yes, I believe he had a breakdown," she said hesitatingly.

"You've heard of the Zeppelin raid last night? Some damage was done on the Coast, a cowardly thing killing innocent people, women and children."

"Oh, I am sorry!" exclaimed Jane. "It is terrible. They must have been near here. Perhaps that is why my husband is leaving."

Spatts smiled as he said:

"It may be the reason. I'll ask him when he comes in."

Jane went out. The sea breeze blew refreshingly; she felt rather faint and it revived her. She did not go direct to the garage but walked along the front; there were few visitors about. She sat down presently. Two men occupied the other end of the seat.

"The police are almost certain the Zeppelins were guided by a motor car. Wish they'd find it," said one of the men.

Jane got up; she could not stand any more of this; she blamed herself for connecting this motor car with Carl. Why did he tell her he had the car repaired at —— and the landlord that he did it himself? She walked back to the hotel very uneasy and found Carl standing at the door with the landlord; they were laughing—this relieved her. Carl turned to her and said:

"Have you packed? We leave after lunch."

She said she had, and asked if he had read about the Zeppelin raid.

"We were just talking about it," he replied.

Spatts went inside, leaving them together.

"The man's a fool," said Carl, jerking his head in the direction of the landlord.

"Is he? What were you laughing at?" asked Jane.

"He said he thought it probable somebody in a motor car guided the airships," said Carl.

"And you think that is not correct?"

"Of course it isn't; how could they do it? I soon proved to him it was not possible, and it was then he laughed at the absurdity of the idea."

"You told me you had the car repaired at ——," she said.

"Well?"

"You told him you did the repairs yourself, in a lonely part of the country."

104

"Don't be a fool, Jane. I don't wish everybody to know where I have been."

"You were at ——?"

"Yes."

"Did you see the airship over there?"

"I saw something hovering in the air but of course I never dreamed it was one of those things."

"And you heard no bombs explode?"

He laughed as he replied:

"Not likely. I should hardly wait for that."

She was not satisfied. When they started on their journey the landlord said:

"I hope you will not have another breakdown, Mr. Meason."

"No fear of that. I've patched it up well; it will carry us to our destination."

"Where's that?"

"Beyond York," said Carl.

"Inquisitive beggar," he said to Jane when the car was away.

"We are not going to York?" she asked.

"No, you asked to go to London; we'll get there to-night," he said.

"Then why did you tell him we were going to York?"

"Because it suited my purpose," he replied.

CHAPTER XXII

JANE SUSPECTS

The journey to London was accomplished without mishap. Carl was a good driver; the car sped along at a rapid pace. Jane enjoyed the ride; the scenery was new to her, and she was observant.

Arriving at the city he drove to the Fairfax Hotel, a quiet place mostly used by families. There was no garage. Leaving Jane there, he went to put up the car.

She waited for him. He seemed a long time coming. She did not care to leave the room in his absence.

At last he came. He made no apology for being away so long; he seemed preoccupied and said little.

They dined together, and then he took her out. The streets were dull and dark, very few lights in the shops, hardly any in the streets. The noise and bustle confused her.

"There's not much to see at night," he said; "we'll have a look round to-morrow."

"What's that?" she asked in alarm.

"A searchlight," he replied laughing. "There's any amount of them but they don't appear to be of much service."

"What are they used for?"

"To discover the whereabouts of Zeppelins."

"It can't be very safe here?"

"It's safe enough; they won't drop bombs near where we are staying."

"How do you know?"

"Oh well, it's not likely; they'll go for something more important than the Fairfax Hotel," he replied.

Jane was tired. They went to bed early. She awoke in the middle of the night and found Carl missing. She thought this strange. There was a dim light burning. She sat up; perhaps he had only gone out of the room, then she noticed his clothes were not there; he had evidently dressed.

She tried to sleep but could not. She was afraid and shivered under the bed-clothes. He had no right to leave her in the hotel at this hour. His actions were mysterious; he always appeared to have something to do in the night. She had no watch and wondered what time it was; then she heard a clock strike one. He must have gone out when she fell asleep.

Soon after she heard an explosion. It sounded some distance away. Then she heard movements in the house, people hurrying about, voices calling. It was strange and disquieting.

Some one paused outside her door; then she heard the handle turn and Carl came into the room, swiftly, silently, closing the door after him and locking it.

She pretended to be asleep, heard him come to the bedside and breathed heavily. He seemed satisfied she did not hear him. He moved away. She opened her eyes and saw him unlocking his suitcase; his back was toward her. He took out some papers, sorted them, put a couple on the dressing-table, then placed the others in the case.

He lit a candle but first turned round and looked at her. She breathed heavily.

She was cautious but she watched him over the top of the clothes, which were drawn up to her face. She was surprised to see him carefully burn the papers. He placed the candle on a newspaper so that the ashes would fall on it. He pressed the pieces with his hand as they fell. When they were consumed he wrapped the remains in a piece of the paper, screwed it tightly, then put the small package in the case. He then undressed and came to the bed.

There was a knock at the door but he made no response. It was repeated, this time louder, sharper.

Carl said in a half-sleepy voice:

"Who's there?"

"It's me, the hall porter; I want to see you for a moment."

Carl got out of bed grumbling. Jane thought he was a long time unlocking the door. She moved restlessly but still pretended to be asleep.

"What is it? Why the deuce do you rouse me at this hour of the night?" asked Carl angrily.

"Mr. Hurd, the manager, said he thought he saw you come into the house a few minutes ago; I said you had not, that you were in your room; I did not see you and I was in the hall."

"Confound him! I shan't stay here if I'm roused up at this unearthly hour. It's abominable! You are disturbing my wife's rest. What are the people tearing about the place for?" asked Carl as he heard footsteps.

"Didn't you hear the explosion? They are at it again."

"Hush!" said Carl. "You'll wake my wife; it will frighten her. You've all gone mad. I heard nothing."

"I'm sorry, sir, but Mr. Hurd was so certain he saw you come in I thought I'd see for myself."

"And what the devil does it matter to him whether I was out or in?" asked Carl sharply.

"That's not my business, sir. Please excuse me. I'll tell him you are in your room," said the man, shuffling away. "Queer smell of burning," he muttered as he went along the landing; "seemed to be in his room."

The manager was in the hall. With him were an inspector of police and a detective.

"Well?" asked Hurd.

"He's in his room, undressed and in bed. I knew he didn't come in."

"You're mistaken," said the Inspector. "He did. I saw him."

"He gave me an accurate description of Mr. Meason," said Hurd, "and I am certain I saw him come in."

The hall porter shook his head.

"I was here when you came downstairs and I didn't see him."

"It's very strange," said the Inspector, looking at the detective. "Are you sure he's the man you followed, that he came in here?"

"We both saw him," said the detective dryly.

"If it is the man, he's been precious quick undressing and getting into bed," said the Inspector doubtfully.

Several people were in the hall. The explosion roused them. They made anxious inquiries; the manager assured them.

Carl Meason listening upstairs little knew what a narrow escape he had. He was not aware he was followed as he hurried back to the hotel nor was he aware that an accurate description of him was in the hands of the police.

It was Valentine Braund, the American millionaire, who had given information to the authorities. He had been to Little Trent the day after Meason left the Sherwood Inn, and a piece of paper found in Carl's room by Abel Head confirmed his suspicions that the man was Karl Shultz who he was convinced was the organizer of the explosion at the Valentine Steel Works. He had asked Head to give him the paper. It did not appear to be of much importance but the name Mannie Kerrnon was written on it. Braund knew this was the woman who worked with Shultz, and his interest became active. He was a determined man and had made up his mind never to forget Shultz. He had already spent money freely trying to find him. He left Head very much mystified and proceeded to interview Tom Thrush.

Thrush recognized him and as usual scented money. Braund proceeded cautiously, asking all sorts of questions about the country, Mr. Chesney, and the stud, also speaking of the two matches at Newmarket which he saw decided.

Tom was completely off his guard and replied with a laugh to his question as to Jane's marriage:

"I don't think she's done amiss. He seems a good sort of man and he has money."

"Well, I hope it will turn out all right," said Braund. "Where did they spend the honeymoon?"

Tom explained. He had heard from Jane. They were at H——.

Braund had some difficulty in restraining his impatience.

"Nice place, isn't it?" he said.

"Quiet, she found it a bit dull; expect they've left by this."

Braund remained with him some little time and then drove away in his motor. He did not return to the Sherwood Inn but told his chauffeur to go the nearest way to H——, "and get there as fast as you can without running into danger."

He soon discovered where Meason and his wife stayed, made inquiries, Frank Spatts gave him every information.

"He was out till nearly three in the morning," said Spatts.

"The night the Zeppelins were over?"

"Yes; he left the next afternoon," said Spatts.

Valentine Braund also discovered that Meason's car had not taken the York road but had traveled London way. He followed quickly and arrived in town not long after Meason. It was Braund who set the police on his track. He was with them when he found they had allowed him to leave the Fairfax Hotel. The Inspector told him they had not sufficient evidence to go upon and were not justified in arresting him.

"You might have stretched a point," grumbled Braund.

"That's all very well. I don't say you're not right, but we have to be very careful in such cases," said the Inspector.

"You are so careful that you allow fellows in motor cars to scour the country and pilot these raiders," snapped Braund.

Carl Meason was alarmed. The police had been informed as to his movements; he had very little doubt about that. He told Jane he must leave London at once, it was very important; he was going to Margate, but she must not tell anybody.

She was disappointed. He had promised to take her about London; she had seen nothing of it.

He answered her sharply. His business was more important than tramping about London.

What was his business, she asked again, and her constant repetition irritated him. He gave no satisfactory replies and she resented this. Jane was sharp, her faculties developed. She was not so simple as he imagined. He was surprised at her persistence. Was she beginning to suspect him? If so what did she think?

The journey to Margate by road was interesting. There was not much conversation. When she spoke he answered in monosyllables. He drove to the White Hart Hotel facing the harbor and engaged a front room.

"You'll be able to pass the time watching the people," he said, "and the harbor is always interesting."

"What shall you be doing?" she asked.

"Don't keep cross-examining me," he replied. "It puts me in a bad temper."

"You are generally in a bad temper," she said.

"Look here, Jane, my girl, we'd better understand each other," he replied. "I have work to do and I mean to carry it out whether you like it or not."

"Are you tired of me already?" she asked.

"Not exactly, but you are going the right way to bring it about," he answered.

"I have a right to know what you are doing."

"Some day if you are very good I may tell you," he said.

Jane became suspicious. The more she was left to herself, the more time she had to think matters over. It seemed strange that Carl was always about where there were Zeppelin raids. She began to connect him with them. Abel Head had called him a spy, perhaps he was, at any rate his movements were suspicious.

The conversations she had heard were disquieting. It was evident several people had doubts about him. She was his wife and she was determined if he did not treat her well not to put up with his conduct. She had money—she took care of that—and she could always go home.

CHAPTER XXIII

ALAN'S DANGER

Eve Berkeley was anxious, having not heard from Alan for several weeks. She eagerly scanned the papers but found no mention of his name. Ella Hallam was with her. Eve was glad of company, it cheered her, and Duncan Fraser came frequently to The Forest, generally looking in at Trent Park on the way.

Eve surmised that Ella was the attraction and hoped that her friend would recognize his many good qualities. She liked Fraser. He did so much for Alan, and the business prospered under his management. He had not heard from him and, like Eve, was growing anxious.

"Perhaps he has been sent on an important mission," he said, "and is unable to write. When he left he hinted at something of the kind."

"The suspense is more than I can bear," she replied.

"I am sure he is safe," said Ella. "Mr. Chesney is capable of taking care of himself."

"Under ordinary circumstances," said Eve; "but there is danger everywhere in France."

Captain Morby was home on leave. He came to see Eve. She welcomed him cordially. Had he any news of Alan?

He looked grave and her heart sank.

"You will keep it secret?" he said.

"Anything you will tell me I will not repeat," she replied.

"He was sent to Brussels," said Harry.

"Brussels!" exclaimed Eve. "Right into the enemy's quarters!"

"Yes, a dangerous mission, but no one so competent to perform it successfully as Alan."

"But Brussels! He will never come out alive!"

Harry smiled as he replied:

"It is part of a great danger, but even if he were discovered I do not suppose his life would be forfeited, although he might be detained."

"Why did he go, who sent him?" she asked.

"A highly placed member of the Belgian Government. I was told on best authority he was specially requested to go," said Harry.

"Then I am not surprised he placed his services at their disposal," said Eve.

"No more am I."

111

It was quite true. Alan had accepted this dangerous mission which, if successfully accomplished, would render great service. He had full permission to go and did not underestimate the risk.

Discarding his uniform he put on civilian clothes and posed as a Belgian. He spoke French fairly well and this helped him. After many narrow escapes he succeeded in reaching Brussels, where he was in danger of discovery every hour. He walked about the streets openly, sat in several cafés, and talked with the people. There were hundreds of German officers and soldiers, but there was nothing particularly suspicious about Alan's appearance. He was well disguised and did not look at all like an Englishman.

Despite this some officers looked at him curiously and in the course of a few days he fancied he was followed.

He succeeded in his mission and learned by heart what he had to say on his return. There were many willing Belgians ready to help him at the risk of their lives. In a fortnight he was ready to leave the city; but this was more difficult than entering it. On every side were Germans, and nobody was allowed to leave Brussels without a special permit, and these were hard to get. He had to wait as patiently as possible for a favorable opportunity. Every day he remained the situation became more dangerous.

So far he had avoided speaking to any of the Englishwomen who were still in the city. He knew he was watched, that the first false step might be fatal.

He did not think there would be much risk in calling at the English nursing home. Many Belgians went there, and he had so far passed as such.

He called, Nurse Ranger received him in her private room. She heard who he was and why he was there. She volunteered to assist him in getting away.

She offered to procure him a permit to leave Brussels, but was afraid it would take some time. When it was secured it would only take him to Bruges or somewhere within the German occupied territory.

Alan said his chief difficulty was to get out of Brussels. Once free from the city he would have a chance of returning to the English lines.

Nurse Ranger was a courageous, a fearless woman, who had rendered valuable assistance to Belgians desirous of joining their comrades in arms.

After some difficulty she procured Alan a permit to leave the city under the name of Armand Roche. This she obtained through a German officer she had nursed back to life and who, for once in a way, proved grateful. Alan did not immediately make use of it.

The permit was countersigned by the Governor and therefore he considered it would frank him anywhere. It expressly stated, however, the limits in which it was available. At last he put it to the test, and arrived as far as Bruges. He had been in the quaint old city before and knew it well. What a contrast to the last time he was there! He recalled it vividly. Now the old market-place was filled with German troops and the hotel where he had formerly stayed tenanted by German officers. It was lucky for him his permit was signed by the Governor of Brussels; he soon found nothing less would have franked him.

The risk would come when he tried to return to his own lines and he prepared for it. All went well. He had a horse provided for him, a fast one that had once been a racer, and he must trust to luck once he got clear of the German lines. How to get clear was, however, a puzzle and he tried to solve it as best he could.

He met one or two German officers who spoke French, and seemed to get on well with them. They were suspicious—he saw that—and of course he did not trust them, but they proved useful as he went about with them. They bragged about their conquests, and Alan urged them on until in their boastfulness they gave him an account of the vast power of the German Army on the Western front and he got valuable information as to the best way to reach the scene of the fighting and the nearest trenches.

He made his attempt to leave Bruges one dark night and had not much trouble in getting out of the town. The danger began when he came to the outskirts and had to pass the cordon drawn round the town to prevent people from leaving in certain directions.

He made the attempt in several quarters and found it too risky; but on this particular night fortune favored him.

It was dark. He rode up to the guard and was challenged. He handed his permit, and when it was being examined he made a bolt into the more open country. For a few precious moments the Germans were surprised and Alan was away in the dark at top speed. The horse was a flyer and no mistake. His heart beat high with hope as he felt it bound under him. Shots were fired but fell short. Then he heard a noise behind him but it was too dark to see anything.

He rode straight ahead, judging this would take him out of the Germans' country. For several hours he went on at a great pace. Occasionally his horse stumbled, but that gave him no anxiety, for he was used to all kinds of situations when riding.

When light began to steal over the landscape he took in the lay of the land. He was in the middle of a wide flat country; the ground was wet and marshy. He had no idea where he was but he seemed safe from pursuit. Not a soul was to be seen. He slowed the horse down to a walk, it was time the animal had a rest.

Where was he?

He went slowly on; then he saw in the distance what looked like a white farm-house. It was a dwelling of some kind and he made for it. As he came within hail an old man stepped out, a Belgian peasant, so Alan judged him by his appearance. He spoke to him in French. The old man regarded him curiously. As Alan looked at him he thought:

"He's a better man than I imagined. Perhaps he's disguised."

In answer to Alan's question he said in excellent French:

"Who are you? You don't look like a civilian."

Alan determined to be straight with him; it would probably be best.

"I am a soldier. I wish to find the English lines."

"Ah!" exclaimed the man. "Get down, come inside. Where are you from?"

"Bruges."

The man held up his hands, tears came into his eyes. He lamented the fall of the city, its occupation by the Germans. He had a daughter in Bruges when the enemy entered the city. He wrung his hands; his grief was painful. He said no more, but Alan guessed and grasped his hands in sympathy—and hate.

Alan put the horse in the tumble-down stable, the roof was half off, the rafters hanging down, the walls crumbling—an old place. It had been in the family of Jean Baptistine for many years. He was a lone man, no wife, three sons fighting, and his daughter— ah well, she was where no harm could come to her. She had saved her honor and sacrificed her life. He was glad of that, very glad, honor was more than life.

He gave Alan food, coarse but clean, which he enjoyed, for he was hungry.

Jean talked freely. He supposed he and his farmhouse were left alone because they were out of the fire zone, or perhaps the barbarians did not think it worth while to meddle with him. There was no wine in the house. He procured a little brandy which he gave to Alan and sipped a small quantity himself.

Alan learned that he was in the enemies' country, that it would be difficult for him to get to the Allied lines. He might be taken at any moment and shot on the spot. He had left his permit in the hands of the guard when he galloped away.

Jean Baptistine said there was no immediate danger. Soldiers did not often come his way. His guest had better lie concealed for a few days. He would be glad of his company, something might happen, the Boches might be driven back defeated.

Alan being tired went upstairs to lie down. The bed was clean, the room smelt fresh. Jean told him to rest comfortably. He threw himself on the bed; before Jean left the room he was asleep.

The sun streaming through the small windows woke him. He sat up, wondering at first where he was.

On the old-fashioned table he saw a pair of gloves and a cigar-case. How came they there?

He got off the bed, took the cigar-case in his hands, and stared in amazement. The monogram V.N. was engraved on it, he recognized it, he had given it to Vincent Newport when he resigned his commission; and Captain Newport was posted among the missing. How came the case here, and the glove?

He was examining them when Jean came up the crazy stairs into the room.

To Alan's rapid question he said:

"He was an officer, he escaped from the escort, they tracked him down. I hid him, but it was no use—they found him."

"What became of him?" asked Alan.

"They took him away," he said. "They would have shot me but he pleaded for me, said I did not hide him, knew nothing about it, that he crept into the house and took the clothes he was wearing himself."

"Then he is alive?" said Alan.

"I believe so. Look," said Jean. He pulled open a drawer and Alan saw in it an officer's uniform.

CHAPTER XXIV

TAKEN PRISONER

It was Vincent Newport's uniform. Alan did not hesitate to use it, he felt he would be safer, as nobody would imagine him to be the man who escaped through the line from Bruges.

Jean raised no objections and Alan gave him the clothes he wore. He offered to guide him to a spot where he might get through the enemy and reach his friends. It would be difficult but there was risk everywhere. Alan protested, if Jean were caught he would be shot, he was sure he could find the way from directions.

"I care little whether they shoot me," said Jean, "my life is ruined."

"It will all come right again after the war," said Alan.

Jean held up his hands, shaking his head despairingly.

"After the war—God knows when that will be," he said sadly.

They started at night. Alan was for leaving the horse behind but Jean said a good steed might save his life.

"It is not fair that you should walk," said Alan. "How far is it?"

"Some thirty miles," said Jean. "That is nothing to me."

They took flasks of brandy and a parcel of eatables. Alan walked with him, leading the horse.

It was a lonely, desolate country, treeless, a barren waste; but Jean loved it. He said the land was better than it looked.

They walked all night. In the early morning they came to an old barn and walked inside with the horse. They were hungry and ate well, a few drops of brandy revived them, some loose hay was given to the horse. A low booming sound was heard, an artillery duel, it continued the greater part of the day. At nightfall Alan mounted his horse and bade good-bye to Jean Baptistine.

"I will hunt you out when we have beaten the Huns," said Alan cheerfully.

"You will beat them," said Jean, "but they are strong, their sins will hang heavy on them when the judgment comes, they are murderers." He cursed them and Alan shivered as he heard what deadly hate there was in the old man's breast. Was it to be wondered at?

Alan rode in the direction of the booming. Jean told him to bear to the right and that would give him more chance of passing the German trenches. He carried his life in his hands but he was cheerful, the sense of danger roused him, the true sporting spirit

116

manifested itself, he was against great odds and meant to succeed. As he went on at a slow pace the heavy firing ceased for a time, then broke out in the occasional boom of a gun. Alan thought they were knocking off for the night; he might have a chance to get through.

As the horse walked along he thought of home and wondered how things were going on at Trent Park and The Forest. It was nearly two months since he had been away from headquarters, and he was not able to write. Eve would be anxious, he must let her know he was safe as soon as possible. He was glad they were not married, it would not have been fair to her; but he vowed she should be his wife if he came safely out of the struggle.

Just before he left for Brussels he had received a letter from Fred Skane in which he said he was preparing Bandmaster for the big steeplechase to be run in Trent Park over a course of four miles. This would be a great event, a sort of Grand National on a small scale. He hoped Alan would be able to come over and ride his horse; he must not forget the date. With the owner up he thought Bandmaster had a chance second to none.

During the excitement and suspense of his journey and stay in Brussels he had forgotten all this but it came to mind now as he rode quietly on toward danger. He remembered the date and began to reckon up, he had lost count during the past few days but he knew there was very little time to spare.

His message delivered, he would have no difficulty in obtaining leave. He hoped to be home in time to ride Bandmaster a few gallops over the course before the race took place.

He gave himself up to pleasant ruminations over his chance of winning until he was rudely roused by a bullet whistling past his ear.

"Snipers about," was his first thought as he set his horse to a gallop.

Another bullet whizzed above his head. He looked round, but saw nobody. It was dark; the sniper must have heard the sound of his horse's hoofs and fired in that direction.

There were only two shots but they roused him out of his reverie and put him on the alert.

Then he wondered how it came about that the sniper was behind the German trenches. Jean told him he would have to pass them somehow. Had he by some strange piece of luck got past the trenches? Was he between two fires? That was hardly possible, yet it might be so.

He pulled his horse up and listened. A strange, buzzing sound was heard—probably some aircraft, although it seemed too dark for aviators to see their whereabouts.

He heard voices and movements of men. A gust of wind carried them toward him. The men spoke German; he had only just stopped in time.

He had no idea where he was. To wait there until daylight would court danger but in which direction ought he to go?

Had he reached a strip of "no man's land," a space left unborrowed and unbroken, lying between two fires? If so he was "between the devil and the deep sea," for he might be fired on by friend and foe alike.

It was a thrilling position, a solitary man on horseback on a dark night on unknown ground and surrounded by enemies. Alan listened with the keen ears of a sportsman, all his faculties alert. A false movement and he was lost.

A scrambling sound close on his left startled him. He fancied it was the men quitting a trench and if so it could only be with one object in view—a night attack. If this were the case it was well planned, for there was very little noise. Alan, however, being near, heard that faint peculiar sound of many men silently on the move.

He would have given much to know where he was—the exact spot. He wondered if old Jean Baptistine had made a mistake and given him wrong directions. He was glad he wore uniform and had Newport's revolver on him—it might be useful.

A faint streak in the sky, a rosy tint wearing down the pale gray, warned him day was breaking and he must be prepared.

There were others waiting for daybreak as well as himself, for the heavy boom of a huge gun sounded quite close at hand. Alan looked in the direction, and saw a cloud of smoke. This was answered by a boom and a cloud from the opposite side and he knew an artillery duel had commenced. Suddenly four men sprang out of a hole formed by a bursting shell. They were Germans. What they were doing there it was impossible to say. They were as surprised to see Alan as he was to see them. In the growing light as he sat on his horse he looked like a phantom emerging out of the mist.

A few minutes passed and the situation was summed up on both sides. A dash was made at Alan, shots fired as he turned his horse to the right and headed right straight at them. His charge was the last thing they expected. He crashed into them, sending two to the ground; the others hung to the horse and saddle.

Alan drew his revolver and shot one man through the head. The horse plunged, reared, but he kept his seat. The two Germans who were knocked down were on him again, but he wrenched free and galloped away. Over this vacant space before him men seemed to spring up like mushrooms. It was impossible to get through and reach the English lines, which he could now see. He made the most of it. His horse faced the situation bravely, but he was pulled out of the saddle and made prisoner. He had narrowly escaped being killed, as sundry bullet tears in his uniform showed. He thanked Heaven he was not in mufti or it would have gone hard with him. He was dragged into the crater-hole from which the four men who had first attacked him emerged. He had killed a man, would they kill him?

A young officer ran up. He looked keenly at Alan, then, in excellent English, asked him his name and regiment. A fire of questions followed as to how he came there and what he was about, why he had left his lines? He was searched but no paper found.

The officer seemed rather a better class man. He ordered Alan to be kept in the hole, and put three men to guard him; then he went away in the direction his men were returning to their trench.

Alan judged there must have been a night attack on the English lines and these were the remnants returning scattered all over the place; if so they must have suffered severely, been almost annihilated.

His guards took very little notice of him. They knew he could not escape; moreover, they had orders to shoot if he attempted it.

It was a dull day and there was very little firing. He judged they were resting after the night attack. It was an awkward fix he was in but nothing daunted he puzzled his brains as to how to get out of it; they had tethered his horse close by—that was in his favor.

The officer did not return, and Alan had nothing to eat or drink—the soldiers did not offer him anything.

Night came on. He wondered whether he would be kept there or removed. At last the young officer came, and with him a soldier carrying a bag which contained food. Alan was handed some, also given a drink, and the officer said he must remain there until next day. If he tried to escape he would be shot. Alan wondered why they did not take him to a more secure spot; something must have happened to prevent this.

He settled himself down, after taking good stock of his position and where the horse was. He pretended to sleep. The three soldiers were left on guard.

They seemed tired, they must have been many hours without sleep. They spoke together in low voices. Presently one of them lay down—it was evident they were to keep guard in turns.

Alan was wide awake and alert now. If he could only make a dash for his horse and spring into the saddle there would be a chance of escaping.

The two men on guard seemed drowsy. The man on the

ground breathed heavily. Alan moved and loosened some stones. The men were alert in a moment and growled at him savagely. Alan waited about an hour—it seemed much longer. He knew exactly where the men were: one on either side, the other still on the ground.

Without a moment's warning he sprang to his feet, let out right and left, and by sheer good luck hit his men hard. He scrambled out of the hole, reached his horse, broke the rope by which it was tied to a stake, cutting his hands as he did so, sprang into the saddle and was galloping away at a great pace before his guard recovered from the shock. They dare not fire for fear of being discovered in the act of letting the prisoner go. The two roused their sleeping comrade, explained the situation, then marched off toward the enemy's lines. They preferred surrender to the death awaiting them if they remained.

CHAPTER XXV

ALIVE AND WELL

Alan was far from being out of the wood, there was danger on every side, and it was light. Fortune favored him, for the enemy had suffered terrible losses and were occupied in beating a hasty retreat, what was left of them. The ground was covered with dead, dying, and wounded. As he rode rapidly to the right he got clear of them; several shots were fired and missed him.

A feeling of exultation possessed him as he neared his lines a couple of miles away. Once there he was safe, his perilous mission accomplished.

His horse shied. Looking ahead he saw half a dozen forms hidden behind some stunted bushes. The enemy again. Rifles were pointed at him. It meant death if he went on.

He halted and faced his enemies, but showed no signs of giving in. The men crept forward, still covering him with their rifles. He was angry at the thought of being taken prisoner again. If recognized he would be shot off-hand. This was not at all likely although he was not aware of it.

Providence intervened in the shape of a shell which hurtled into the midst of the creeping men. There was a terrific explosion. Alan reeled in the saddle, recovered by a great effort, and managed to control his frightened horse. He was struck on the forehead but fortunately the peak of his cap saved him. Still the effect was stunning, stupefying. A whistling in the air and another shell burst, throwing up a cloud of mud and dirt round him, thus lessening the danger of being badly hit.

His enemies were cut up, shattered; but he had to ride for his life to avoid the shells. He was in danger from his friends.

The horse was equal to the emergency and sped across the open space at a great pace.

The solitary horseman seemed to puzzle the gunners, for they ceased firing. Probably he had been recognized as an officer escaping from the enemy.

He waved his cap and, taking all risks, galloped toward the Allies' lines. He knew where he was now. These trenches were the nearest to headquarters and in a few minutes he would be in safety.

Something trickled down his face. He brushed it aside with his hand—blood—his wound was more serious than he thought.

121

His left arm pained—blood on the sleeve. His left thigh twinged sharply—there was blood here also.

"Must have had a narrow squeak," he thought. He felt faint, inclined to swoon, but held on to his horse firmly.

His head swam, his sight grew dim, he heard a roar from the front trench and then—oblivion.

When he came to he was being attended behind the firing line. He wondered where he was, and tried to sit up, but fell back exhausted. The doctor told him to keep still.

He slept several hours. When he awoke he was in the ambulance, jolting farther away from the line.

It was twenty-four hours or more before he was able to stand. Once on his legs he quickly recovered and, asking for his horse, which was near at hand, declared his intention of riding to headquarters.

The doctor protested; but when Alan explained who he was and the nature of his mission no further objections were raised.

"You have had a marvelous escape," said the doctor, looking at him admiringly. "You are a brave man."

Alan smiled as he thanked him, saying there would have been many officers who would have been glad of the chance to take his place and run the risks.

He rode to headquarters and was heartily welcomed. In a few moments he stood before his chief, who held out his hand, shook his heartily, and congratulated him.

It was then Alan learned it had been reported that he was shot in Bruges as a spy. No doubt this report had been made in order to save the men responsible for his escape through the lines.

"Shot as a spy," thought Alan. "I wonder if it has been made public in England. If so, what a terrible shock to Eve and all my friends."

He suppressed his feelings and gave an account of how he fulfilled his mission.

"You must see King Albert at once," said the chief. "It was a blow to him when he heard you were shot."

The news of Captain Chesney's return was soon noised abroad, and on all sides he was congratulated.

He hunted up Skane's letter and found the date of the Trent Park Grand Steeplechase would give him ample time to get home and ride Bandmaster over the course two or three times. He must see about his leave at once.

He supposed his safe arrival would be at once reported at home and that Eve would see it and others.

There was a budget of letters for him some six weeks old. One of the last he opened came from his trainer. The date of the Steeplechase had been altered because the troops camped in the Park had left earlier than was expected.

Alan was uncertain about the date. He asked, and found he had just a couple of days to spare to get there in time.

Then came another thought which made him gasp. Had Bandmaster been struck out when he was reported shot?

Every minute was precious.

He wired to Skane at once, imposing secrecy, and asking it Bandmaster was still in the race. If so he would be home to ride.

"Not a word about this."

Fred Skane had not scratched Bandmaster. He would not believe Alan Chesney had been shot, and this firm conviction cheered Eve Berkeley wonderfully. Then came the news that Captain Chesney had returned to headquarters after many hairbreadth escapes and that he was severely wounded.

The reaction set in at Trent Park, The Forest, and Little Trent. Gloom turned to joy; everybody was gay and festive. Captain Chesney was safe, he would soon recover from a few wounds, these were trifles to a brave strong man.

"There you are," said Fred Skane. "What did I tell you, Miss Berkeley. I knew he was not shot—not likely. Supposing I'd scratched Bandmaster—there'd have been a row and no mistake. 'Scratch the horse out of respect,' says Abel Head. 'Memory,' says I, 'what memory? He's alive. There's no memory about Captain Chesney yet, I'll bet, or I'm a Dutchman.'"

Eve laughed.

"Splendid, Fred, splendid! You were right; we were all wrong. But he was reported shot."

"Reported be——" said Fred, checking himself. "Who believes reports? Not me! We get too much or too little, and it came from a German source; not good enough, says I, not half good enough for this child."

When the trainer received Alan's telegram he chuckled, then laughed heartily.

"By Jove, this is grand! Won't there be a double distilled surprise for 'em all. If he can get home—if? He must!—and ride, wounds or no wounds—and he'll win, I can see him doing it—what a day it will be! Not a word, not me; I wouldn't miss the shock of his appearance on the course, in an unexpected way, not for a thousand."

"Fred's a bit above himself," said Abel Head. "He's confounded cheeky because his opinion has turned out correct. I never thought Captain Chesney was shot, did you?"

"No," said Tom Thrush, "not likely."

"And Fred takes it all on himself. He goes about with his 'What did I tell you?' until I'm sick of hearing it," said Abel.

"The main thing is, the master's alive; nowt else matters," said Tom.

"Heard from Jane lately?" asked Abel.

"No; can't make it out," said Tom gloomily.

"I hope it's all right with her. You were a fool to let her marry him," said Abel.

"What's the sense in pitching that into me now?" growled Tom.

"I pitched it into you before it was too late, but you took no notice."

"Do you always follow good advice?" asked Tom.

"Maybe not, not always."

"Then dry up about me. I'm sorry, Abel, sorry for my lass; but he'd best behave well to her or he'll know about it," said Tom savagely.

"Where are they?"

"Don't know; haven't heard from her since they left Margate."

"I'll tell you another thing, Tom. It's what I've always said, Carl Meason's a German spy and it's my belief Jane's found him out."

"If that's so and she has you can lay she'll give him away, it's her duty to do it," said Tom.

"Probably she will if he gives her a chance," was Abel's reply.

"What chance? He can't interfere with her."

"There's no telling what a man like that will do," answered Abel.

To return to Alan Chesney, he was anxious in the extreme. His wounds troubled him but he endeavored to shake off the feeling. He had no wish to be invalided at home. He wanted the change on his own account and for a particular purpose, to ride Bandmaster in the Steeplechase. He applied for leave, which was readily granted, and was ordered not to return until quite well.

He told two or three of his brother officers why he was anxious to get home and of course they were determined to have "a bet on" Bandmaster. His servant heard the news and it quickly got about among the rank and file.

A vexatious delay occurred—one of those small but important matters to be attended to at the last minute which are forever turning up at important moments.

Alan motored to Calais; and here again there was delay, no steamer being available for several hours. He fretted and fumed

124

about. If this sort of thing continued there would be little chance of being home in time to see the race, let alone ride.

He passed a restless time but at last the boat started and he was fairly on the way. All being well he would reach Little Trent in good time on the morning of the meeting.

None of his friends knew he was coming except Fred Skane, the trainer. His brief telegram to Eve said nothing about it. She was overwhelmed with joy to hear from him that he was really safe and well.

Being a sensible woman she determined to celebrate Alan's good news by taking a large party of friends to Trent Park to see Bandmaster win. Fred Skane said to her:

"I think he'll win, but I wish Captain Chesney was here to ride him. It would be 'a cert' then."

CHAPTER XXVI

THE RIDER IN KHAKI

A splendid four-mile was planned out at Trent Park, a real test for chasers, almost up to the famous Aintree Grand National journey. There were stiff fences, two water jumps, some plough lane, and excellent going on grass. The horse that won would be a good 'un.

Bandmaster had done a great preparation. The trainer did not spare him; he had been over the course three or four times.

Sam Kerridge's son Will was to ride in the event of Captain Chesney's not being able to do so.

It was a clear, bright, sharp morning, and from an early hour motors and buses came by road. There was every promise of a big gathering even without the use of train service. Keen sportsmen were not to be denied the pleasure of such a meeting by any inconveniences they might have to put up with.

Eve Berkeley and her house party arrived in good time. Duncan Fraser was one, he attached himself to Ella Hallam. She could not fail to notice he was attracted. She liked him, his sterling worth appealed to her and Eve was always singing his praises.

Bernard Hallam was friendly with him. He was not at all displeased to notice Fraser and Ella were on excellent terms. He was partial to keen business men and such an one was Duncan Fraser.

There were three events before the Trent Grand Steeplechase, but the chief interest was centered in the big event, on which there was a lot of wagering.

Baron Childs was running Handy Man, a formidable steeplechaser who had missed the Grand National by an ace on two occasions. He was fully expected to make amends for two unlucky seconds at Aintree.

There was an interval of nearly an hour between the third event and the Steeplechase. The time was occupied in wagering and looking at the twenty-seven runners.

Bandmaster was favorite, the popularity of his owner had much to do with this. An official account of Alan's mission to Brussels had been made public, and he was the hero of the hour; much was given out but it was guessed more remained to be disclosed.

Apart from this, Bandmaster was regarded as a great horse. If half as good over a steeplechase course as on the flat he must possess a great chance. His speed was undeniable. If he proved a safe jumper nothing would be able to live with him on the flat at the finish. Fred Skane's opinion was known. The trainer had little fear of defeat. He said confidently that Bandmaster would carry the brown and blue to victory.

Eve Berkeley never looked better. Her cheeks glowed with health. She was happy—Alan was safe, what else mattered? She was radiant. Baron Childs did not conceal his admiration. She wore costly furs; they became her well. She walked proudly because of her hero, the man of the hour, the bravest of the brave.

There was only one thing lacking. If Alan could have ridden Bandmaster how glorious it would have been.

The party from The Forest caught her enthusiasm and exuberance of spirits. Their merry laughter rang clear and joyous.

Captain Morby was there, paying a flying visit from the front to see Bandmaster win. He had not met Alan since his return from his adventure.

It was half an hour before the race and a bustling scene took place as the twenty-seven horses were put to rights.

Riders hurried across the enclosure, stopping to speak to friends, colors just showing through the half-open coats, for the air was nipping. Most of them were gentlemen jockeys, five or six officers who had won their spurs over stiff courses and had capped this by brave actions at the front. Everybody recognized that racing, sport generally, had much to do with the wonderful heroism displayed in the war.

Will Kerridge was anxious. He hoped Bandmaster would win. He wanted the ride badly, but would have stood down gladly to let Alan Chesney have the mount. Fred Skane said nothing to him about Alan's intention to arrive home in time to have the ride on his horse. He was glad he had not mentioned it now; he thought Alan was detained, that he had not sufficiently recovered from his wounds to bear the journey.

A quarter of an hour more it was hopeless to expect him and yet even now Fred did not quite give up hope.

He looked anxiously about, raised his glasses and fixed them on the road from Trent Park house. Nobody was coming. After all, Kerridge must ride—and win. He had given particular instructions how Bandmaster was to be handled. The riding of the horse had been discussed at the stud groom's house on several occasions. Sam was very anxious his son should win.

While the bustle and excitement was at its height at Trent Park a powerful motor car was speeding along the high-road at top pace. The driver was experienced and working under pressure, he had been promised a liberal tip if he arrived in time.

Behind sat Alan, endeavoring to restrain his feelings and keep quiet. From time to time he looked at his watch and replaced it in his pocket with an impatient movement.

The car stopped with a jerk. The driver was out in a moment. Alan followed. What was wrong?

The tool box was relied upon. The man knew his work. In a quarter of an hour the car moved on, but precious time had been lost.

"We'll do it all right," said the driver.

Alan doubted, but held his peace. It would be a terrible disappointment to arrive too late.

He must keep as calm as possible, excitement was bad for him, his nerve had been severely tried.

The landscape became more familiar with each mile passed. He was lucky to be home again. He gave a few thoughts to his recent adventures and was thankful he had pulled through.

The Park appeared in the distance. A glance at the watch showed it would be "neck or nothing," he might just do it.

Something went wrong with the steering gear, the car swerved and the front wheels stuck in the ditch. The driver was shot out and Alan flung against the back of the front seat. The man was unhurt and on his feet in a few seconds.

Alan swore; he could not help it.

"Lost by a few seconds," he said.

"I'll have her out," said the driver, who was in the car. By much display of skill and force he backed it out, fixed the steering gear, and said:

"Get in, sir, we'll do it yet. Is that the course?" and he pointed to where the flags waved.

"That's it," said Alan excitedly.

"Is the going on the grass good?"

"Yes."

"Then I'll steer straight for it."

The car bounded over the turf with occasional jumps. Alan held on to the seat, no chance, the race was timed for three-thirty. The horses must be going out. He hoped they would be late. Probably there were many runners, a big field, and the weighing facilities improvised for the occasion would not conduce to rapidity.

Fred Skane took a final sweep over the Park through his glasses. He saw the car, guessed who it was and, calling to Will Kerridge not to go out on to the course for a minute, made a bolt to the entrance gate.

The car pulled up quickly. Alan sprang out.

"You, Fred, am I in time?" he said.

"Just follow me," replied Fred as he ran toward the weighing room.

"Get into the scales. Eleven stone," he yelled, then bolted to find the stewards.

There was a hurried consultation. Major Daven consulted for a few minutes, then went to the weighing room.

"God bless me—Chesney! This is a surprise," he gasped.

"Can I ride Bandmaster?" asked Alan breathlessly.

"Yes, of course; I'll tell 'em. They're not all out yet. God bless my soul, this is a surprise! How do you feel?" said the Major, giving out orders between gasps, sending attendants flying in all directions.

"No time to change; I'll have to ride in khaki," said Alan.

"And there's no better color," said the Major.

"How about the weight?" said the trainer, stumbling and gasping.

"All right; two pounds over weight," said the clerk of the scales.

"Declare it," said Fred.

"Two pounds over," shouted the Major; "up with it on the board, owner up, don't stand there gaping. Bandmaster's the horse—fly! God bless my soul, what a surprise it will be!"

Alan pitched his cap in a corner.

"You've spurs on, don't use them."

"All right," said Alan.

"And I say, mind the water jumps—they're stiff."

"All right," said Alan as he was rushing out, the trainer on his heels shouting hints and instructions.

"Something's causing delay," said the Baron, noticing three or four horses still in the paddock.

Eve looked.

"Bandmaster is still there," she said, "and Kerridge has dismounted."

"There's a regular bustle round the weighing room," said Harry Morby.

They saw attendants running in and out and Fred Skane hurriedly appearing, making for Bandmaster.

A buzz of excitement rose; inquiries were made; a feeling of suspense was in the air.

A man climbed up to the number board. Eve saw him.

"A rider changed at the last minute," she said.

Then she noticed Will Kerridge's name taken out and her

129

heart almost stopped beating. She trembled, became pale with excitement.

"Good Lord, what's up?" exclaimed Mr. Hallam. "Shall I go and find out?"

"No occasion," said Harry excitedly. "Look!"

A khaki-clad figure, a soldier in officer's uniform, much worn and travel-stained, with no cap, came tearing out of the weighing room and across the paddock to where Bandmaster stood.

"By all that's wonderful, it's Alan!" exclaimed Duncan Fraser.

"Yes, yes!" said Eve, and felt on the verge of fainting. She could hardly believe her eyes. It was Alan sure enough, marvelous. How had he got there? She quivered with the tumult of her feelings. The surprise was too much for her, the exquisite joy of seeing him again overcame her.

Alan shook hands hurriedly with Will Kerridge.

"Sorry to take the mount from you, Will," he said with a smile.

"You're welcome, Captain; I'm right glad you came in time," was the reply.

Alan mounted and rode Bandmaster on to the course.

"Who is the rider in khaki?" asked a well-known man.

"Blest if I know. He's riding Bandmaster too." He turned to look at the board.

"Well, of all the wonderful things!" he exclaimed. "It's Captain Chesney, the owner; he must have just arrived from the front in time."

CHAPTER XXVII

THE STEEPLECHASE

Alan was recognized by scores of people, deafening cheers greeted his appearance on Bandmaster. He walked the horse past the stand and saw Eve and her friends. Stopping for a moment he waved his hand. There was a flutter of handkerchiefs in response. Eve was a proud woman. Her hero, everybody's hero, was there sitting his horse well, eager for the fray, ready to show how he could ride.

The horses were at the post as he cantered down. The starter wondered why the favorite was late. He could not let them go without him.

The riders looked at the khaki-clad horseman and some of them recognizing him cheered wildly.

"It's Captain Chesney," said Dan Rowton, rider of Handy Man.

When he came up there was a general cheer and many of them expressed pleasure that he was riding. There was no time to talk. Alan smiled his thanks and took his place in the center. In a minute or two they were off, Frosty going away with the lead.

Alan's feelings can be imagined. He was excited, small wonder at it. He thought how wonderful that he was there in Trent Park, riding in the steeplechase.

The tension of the motor ride against time strung him to the highest possible pitch and he had not quite recovered from his wounds.

How glorious it was to be on Bandmaster! How much had happened since the horse won the Hunt Cup! Many startling events had crowded one another in rapid succession.

Bandmaster moved well. Alan was already on good terms with his mount. The first fence was reached, not a formidable obstacle. All the horses got over but three or four jumped wildly. Bandmaster flew it like a bird.

There were three spills before the stand was reached. As they swept past there was much cheering. Bandmaster's rider was singled out for a tremendous reception as the horse cleared the stiff fence in grand style.

The rider in khaki looked conspicuous among the bright-colored racing jackets—hatless, his uniform well worn.

They swung round the bend, then entered some ploughed land which found out the weak spots. Two fields were crossed and the first water jump reached. There was a wide ditch in front of the high fence; the water gleamed in the bright light.

Frosty refused and whipped round, causing three more to swerve out. True Blue stopped short, then sprang into the water, where he remained, much to the annoyance of many riders, but they managed to steer clear. Alan let Bandmaster go. The horse made a grand leap, landing safely. He was delighted at the performance and his hopes of winning were high. The pace was strong, testing the power of the horses and already a dozen were hopelessly out of it.

From the stand there was a good view of the race and when Eve saw Bandmaster clear the water jump in gallant style she cheered.

"Beautifully done," said the Baron. "Captain Chesney has a real good horse under him."

He noticed Eve's heightened color and how excited she was. Her eyes flashed and sparkled; there was more than ordinary interest in them. He wondered if Captain Chesney were first favorite.

"He is a splendid rider," said Eve.

"None better," said Captain Morby.

"He's handicapped heavily," said Mr. Hallam. "It will be extraordinary if he can last out such a severe race after all he has gone through."

"Wonderful pluck," said Duncan Fraser. "Always had."

"I want to hear how he arrived in time. It will be interesting. He must have had a race for it," said Ella.

"And won on the post. I hope he'll win this race," said Duncan.

The horses were almost out of sight as they passed some trees but the colors could be seen dodging between them. When they were in full view again Handy Man led, with Milkmaid, Picket, Fright, and Sparrow close behind. Bandmaster came next, alone, followed by the rest. Seven had fallen and there was a long tail.

Handy Man was a grand jumper and Dan Rowton a good rider. The pair seemed to get on well. So far the horse had not made a mistake.

The last mile and a half was a severe test, the jumps being all stiff, and the pace began to tell.

A thorn hedge faced the field at this point. Handy Man flew it safely, so did Milkmaid, Fright, and Sparrow, but Picket came down with a crash, rolled over, flung his rider out of danger, and was struggling to rise as Alan on Bandmaster came along. It was an awkward, dangerous situation; a less experienced horseman might have lost his head. Alan, however, was accustomed to act quickly in emergencies. He pulled his mount to the left and just cleared the struggling horse. Picket, however, was so near Bandmaster that he put him out of his stride; this caused loss of ground and he fell back.

Eve noticed the danger and gave a slight cry of alarm, followed by a sigh of relief as she saw Bandmaster safe.

"A narrow squeak," said Harry. "Nobody but a good rider would have escaped."

The pace was tremendous, considering a mile had to be covered, and not more than ten of the twenty-seven starters were within striking distance.

It was a formidable mile to the winning post, a stiff fence, then the water jump, bigger than the first, and two hurdles brushed in the straight, the last being close to the winning post.

Alan felt faint but kept hard at it. He was not so strong as he thought. His wounds and all he had gone through sapped his strength. He possessed indomitable courage, a stubborn will which stood him in good stead.

Bandmaster tipped the first fence but it did no harm and he raced after Handy Man, Milkmaid, and Sparrow at his best pace.

The water jump loomed in front a formidable obstacle. Handy Man scrambled over, narrowly escaping a fall. Alan thought the Baron's horse was about done. Sparrow fell. Milkmaid cleared it well. Alan had a clear course and steadied his mount. Once over the water he had a great chance, for on the flat Bandmaster had tremendous pace. His eyes were misty, he could not see clearly, his head swam, something trickled down his leg; the wound in his thigh had opened and was bleeding. He felt Bandmaster rise under him, knew he was in the air over the water, topped the fence, and came down safely; but it was almost a miracle he did not fall off, he swayed in the saddle, it was only by a tremendous effort he retained his seat. Bandmaster was a wonder. Alan was not able to give him any assistance at the jump.

The easy going on the flat gave him a chance but his eyes were dim and his head ached. The reins were loose in his hands.

From the stand it was easy to see there was something wrong with the rider in khaki, and Eve became very anxious. Rapidly she thought of all Alan had gone through and wondered if it were telling on him. If so would he be able to ride his horse out, handle him skillfully over two rather treacherous hurdles, they were the easiest jumps in the course to look at.

Everybody was excited. Alan's condition was palpable, he seemed suddenly to have lost his strength and with it the control of his mount.

Fred Skane looked on aghast. He knew the danger better than any one. If Alan was spent, Bandmaster might blunder and there would be a nasty spill. He hoped for the best as he watched with his feelings strung to the highest pitch.

Handy Man, Milkmaid, and Bandmaster were running in the order named as the first of the two hurdles was reached. The Baron's horse was tiring fast, and Milkmaid had about enough of it. Bandmaster traveled well but did not gain much ground.

All three scrambled over, their style being slovenly, quite different from the early part of the race.

Alan swayed in the saddle, then bent forward. It seemed every minute as though he must fall off. It was a terrible strain on him after all he had gone through.

Eve was trembling with the intensity of her feelings, expecting every moment to see him collapse—what mattered losing the race if he escaped unhurt?

Backers of the favorite were anxious. They sympathized with Alan, at the same time thought it would have been better had young Kerridge been allowed to ride.

As they raced up to the last hurdle every eye was fixed on the horses. Handy Man stumbled on to his knees as he landed, but Dan Rowton cleverly kept his seat, made a fine recovery, set his mount going again, and was deservedly applauded. Milkmaid landed clumsily, staggering along for the winning post—-beaten but in front.

Bandmaster, with the reins loose in Alan's hands, pricked up his ears and took off too soon. There was a moment of intense suspense; then, as the horse crashed into it, Alan seemed to be roused to make a supreme effort. He clutched the reins, held Bandmaster together, and stopped a bad fall; the hurdle was knocked down but the horse retained his feet. All three were tired but Bandmaster had most go in him for a run on the flat. By degrees he overhauled Milkmaid, who had fallen back, and passing her went in pursuit of Handy Man.

The race became desperately exciting. Alan appeared to have had a relapse after his momentary rousing, and gave Bandmaster no help. It was painful for Eve to watch him. As she looked she saw a red splash on the khaki breeches and exclaimed:

"He's hurt! There's blood on him!" then sank backward. The Baron steadied her in time. It was hardly a faint; she felt dizzy, and quickly recovering thanked him.

Bandmaster ran his own race. He seemed to know what was required, it was exciting to watch him.

Nearer and nearer he drew to Handy Man and Rowton had to ride hard. The odds were in favor of the Baron's horse but

Bandmaster, despite all disadvantages, stuck to his guns and at last reached his girth.

The cheering was loud, it gave encouragement to Alan, he sat up in the saddle and urged his mount to make a final effort.

It was just in time; another moment and Handy Man, driven hard by Dan, would have won.

Bandmaster drew level. The pair were head and head for a couple of strides. The crowd watched breathlessly, too excited to cheer for the moment.

The winning post was only a few yards ahead. Alan saw it dimly and held on to his work with grim determination.

Bandmaster's head was in front, then his neck, in another stride he was half a length to the good. As he passed the post in front of Handy Man cheering broke out wildly.

CHAPTER XXVIII

JANE'S DISCLOSURES

It was a sensational finish. As Alan rode in he hardly knew where he was or what had happened. He managed to get out of the saddle, unbuckle the girths and carry it into the weighing room. He sank into the scale; when "all right" was declared he staggered to his feet, outside they were waiting for him.

The crowd stood back, making way for Eve Berkeley and her friends. She went quickly to Alan, took his arm firmly, Duncan Fraser the other side helped him to limp along. The cheering was deafening, but Alan did not notice it. When Eve spoke he made no reply.

It was evident he was not in a condition to remain on the course. Eve insisted upon taking him to The Forest in her motor; she said there would be more comfort than at Trent Park because he was not expected home.

Alan was helped into the motor in a dazed condition. Eve and Duncan Fraser went with him, She had her arm in his, pressing it sympathetically, but he did not seem to be aware of it, or know where he was. Before they arrived at The Forest he was asleep, they had some difficulty in rousing him.

In the dining-room he went straight to the sofa, threw himself down heavily, and was asleep in a moment.

"He's tired out," said Eve, placing her hand on his head. "He will be better for a rest. We must take care the others do not wake him when they return."

They covered him with rugs. Duncan Fraser remained in the room while Eve went to telephone for the doctor, who on his arrival said sleep was the best possible thing for him and he must on no account be disturbed.

Alan slept until the next morning, Harry Morby remaining in the room all night. When he awoke he remained quite still for some time, wondering where he was and what had happened. Had he been ill? If so how long? No recollection of the race came to him; he fancied he was at headquarters, but the surroundings were strange—much more luxurious.

Captain Morby was asleep in the armchair; he had been awake most of the night. Alan saw him as he lay on the sofa and recognized him. What was Harry Morby doing here? He was not on the staff. Perhaps he had been promoted. Gradually his faculties became cleared. The sleep had done good, his brain worked, the dull sensation vanished. He sat up. As he did so, Harry Morby awoke.

"Better, old chap?" he asked with a smile. Then he noticed Alan looking round and went on:

"Don't know where you are, eh? I'll enlighten you. You're at The Forest, the home of that most beautiful lady, Evelyn Berkeley. You're a fortunate man to have won her sympathy so completely. By Jove, old man, you rode a great race yesterday! But you were clean done up at the finish and no wonder."

"What the deuce are you doing here?" asked Alan.

"I'm home for a few days, made up my mind to see Bandmaster win the steeplechase."

"And did he?" asked Alan.

"Did he! I should rather think so. Don't you remember?" said Harry.

"I have some recollection of a race. Did I ride him?"

"Of course you did, but it took you all your time to stick on at the finish."

"I remember," said Alan. "I was pretty right till I got to the last water jump. I don't recollect much after that."

"No, I don't suppose you do. You were certainly dazed when you dismounted."

"And he really won?"

"He did."

"Bandmaster is a great horse, a wonderful horse," said Alan enthusiastically. "I didn't help him a bit; he won the race on his own. Tell me all about it."

Captain Morby, nothing loath, gave a good description of the race. Alan listened attentively, as though it were the first he had heard of it.

"It was a race to get there in time," said Alan, and described hurriedly how he came from France and motored to the course. He stood up, looked at himself in the glass, and said:

"I'm a nice object. I want cleaning up. I'm smothered in dirt and dust. What time is it?"

"Half-past six."

"Then we'll scrub before they're up. How did I get here?"

Harry told him and added:

"Miss Berkeley left me on guard for the night. I believe she wanted to remain but thought it better not."

"Come along," said Alan. "I'm for a tub; I feel a heap better now, it's good to be home again after all I've gone through."

"You'll have to tell us about your adventures," said Harry.

"It's a long story; by Jove, old fellow, I wonder I'm alive!" said Alan.

Eve Berkeley was down in good time, anxious to learn how Alan was. She found the door open, looked in, there was nobody in the room. She rang the bell.

"Have you seen Captain Chesney?" she asked.

Johnson smiled.

"He's in the bathroom," he said.

"You have seen him?"

"I met him on the stairs."

"What did he say?"

"'How are you, Johnson? I'm going down for a tub. It will take some time to get clean, but I'll try and be down for breakfast. I'm hungry.'"

"That was all?"

"Yes."

"Did he look ill?"

"No, a bit tired. He's a wonderful man."

"He is, Johnson; you are quite right, a very wonderful man," said Eve with a bright smile.

When Alan came down he found her in the morning-room. He held out his arms.

"Come to me, Eve, come! I want you badly—I love you so. I thought once I should never see you again and it nearly killed me. I dreaded the idea of never seeing you more than the danger or the bullets."

She came; he took her to him and kissed her passionately. Johnson discreetly closed the door, he was an admirable servant. They were alone for an hour, a blessed time, more united than they had been, their hearts beating in unison; they were one.

Hurriedly he gave her a brief outline of his adventures. She listened breathlessly. He was indeed a hero, a brave man, and he was hers; her happiness was almost too much, she simply sighed and nestled to him. He punctuated his tale with kisses. He ended by saying in determined tones:

"We must be married before I return. I can't risk it again, after all I have gone through. I dare not. You will consent, Eve; you will?"

She said yes and he was soothed and satisfied.

"Perhaps it will be as well to tell them all at breakfast," she said.

"All who?"

She laughed and gave him the names of her guests.

"What an ordeal!" he said. "Who will tell them?"

"You must, Alan, and spare my blushes."

Not much surprise was manifested when Alan made the announcement. There was a chorus of congratulations; everybody thought it an excellent match. Captain Morby said to himself:

"I knew they'd do it, but they have been a long time about it."

Alan had to relate his adventures in Brussels and Bruges. He thrilled his listeners as he described his hair-breadth escapes on his return to headquarters.

He was not due back for a few weeks; during that time he and Eve were quietly married at Little Trent Church, only a few persons being present. They went for a brief honeymoon to the South and on their return to Trent Park met with a great reception.

Mr. Hallam arranged with Eve to remain at The Forest until his return to Australia. He seemed in no hurry to leave England.

It was during Alan's stay at Trent Park that Jane Meason surprised her father by returning home alone.

"I have left him," she said. "He has behaved shamefully; he is a spy. I have found him out. I will never live with him again."

"What's he done?" said Tom gloomily.

"Many things. Abel Head was quite right: he is in the pay of the Germans; I can prove it," said Jane.

She was reticent and Tom did not get much information from her. He found out, however, that Carl had threatened her if she disclosed anything about his work or what he was doing.

"What did he say?" asked Tom.

"He told me if I got him into trouble he would do for me," said Jane.

"We'll see about that," answered Tom angrily. "Threatened your life, did he? Well, he'll have me to deal with first."

Jane did not show any alarm at her husband's threats; for one thing she did not believe in them. He might risk coming to find her at Little Trent Park, at least she thought so.

Tom told Alan what his daughter said.

"I'll see her," he said, "and find out all about him. We'll put a spoke in his wheel before long; if he's caught red-handed he'll be shot and she will be well rid of him."

"The Government ought to reward her," said Tom.

Alan smiled; Tom was after the money again.

"I have no doubt she will be recompensed for what she has gone through," he said.

Eve sent for Jane to come to Trent Park and persuaded her to tell Alan what she knew. This she was willing to do; Alan was different from her father, he was a soldier and had a right to know.

Jane stated that Carl Meason had signaled to the raiders from his motor car. She had no doubt about it; he did so when they left

Margate. She was sure of it now although at the time he gave a plausible explanation as to why he showed two such large bright lights. She knew the Zeppelins were guided by the signals he flashed; when she found out she was frightened but later on after a quarrel she taxed him with it. Carl was in a terrible rage, she thought he would have struck her. His threats daunted her for a time and she kept quiet, but when she read about the murderous bombs and destruction of innocent lives she determined to disclose all she knew at the proper time.

Alan and Eve listened to her story. They had no doubt as to its truth. Carl Meason must be caught. Had she any idea where he was? She had not but expected he would seek her out at the cottage. She had left him a note in which she said she was going home and would never live with him again. She handed Alan a document she had taken from his case before she left. It clearly implicated him; there was no doubt he had been in the pay of the enemy for months, that he had mapped out raids for them, organized a system of spying in England.

"This is sufficient to condemn him," said Alan. "You really think he will dare to seek you here?"

Jane said she felt sure of it.

"Then we'll watch for him. He shall not escape," said Alan, but he was doubtful if Carl Meason would run his head into a hornets' nest.

CHAPTER XXIX

A SPLASH IN THE DARK

Carl Meason was angry because Jane left him, but he did not think she would betray him. He was well paid for his villainy: large remittances reached him by a round-about route. He was flush of money. He was lost without Jane. She appealed to him. He did not love her but he wanted her; she was his and he meant to get her back.

There would not be much risk in going to Trent Park, he thought. He had warned her he would be dangerous if she gave him away, that she would come to harm; she seemed frightened by his threats. It was not likely she would brave them.

He understood why she left him, or thought so; it was because she knew he undertook risks and might suffer as his accomplice if they were caught.

"She'll have to come away with me," he said. "I'll square her father; it's only a matter of cash."

It was some time after she left him he decided to take her away. He wrote; she had not answered his letters. He cursed her for an obstinate jade, vowing he would pay her out.

Jane showed her father his letters and he duly reported to Alan, who ordered a watch to be kept round the Park and near the cottage. Abel Head, Tom Thrush and several of the men at Trent Park were special constables. They thought it would be a feather in their cap if they caught a spy.

Carl Meason was cunning. He wished to find out how the land lay before venturing there. He sent one of his confidential agents to make inquiries. He returned in a couple of days, saying there were men about, watching the place, evidently on the lookout for somebody.

From this Carl gathered Jane had given information against him and flew into a terrible rage. Come of it what might he decided to punish her even if he ran risks.

He made elaborate preparations for his journey, hired a small but powerful car, disguised himself thoroughly. He was an adept at making up. In New York he had more than once saved his life owing to his skill. He knew the country well. He journeyed down in the daytime, passing through Little Trent slowly, saw Abel Head at the door of the Sherwood Inn, smiled as he noticed he was unrecognized. He went at the same pace along the road leading past the wall where the door opened near Tom Thrush's cottage.

Jane heard the motor, opened the door, and looked out. So well was he disguised that she failed to recognize him or the car.

Motorists often went through the road in Trent Park and no notice was taken of Meason and his car.

It so happened that Alan and his wife were in London and as there had been no signs of Meason the watchers relaxed their vigilance. Tom Thrush was of opinion Meason had cleared out because he was in danger of being discovered; and Abel Head was of the same mind.

Jane felt safer. Perhaps he divined she had told of his doings and in consequence he thought it safer to hide for a time. She was, however, careful not to go far away from home, nor did she walk outside the Park. There was no telling what a desperate man would do.

Fortune favored Carl Meason. The night was dark, misty; a dense white stream covered the park, strangely thick and wetting. Leaving his motor under the wall some distance from the door where it was hidden by creepers overhanging, he concealed himself in one of the thick embrasures and watched. He was well protected by his motor coat, light but warm and water-proof.

He looked at his wrist watch. The illuminated figures showed it was eight o'clock. He wondered at the pitchy blackness of the night, unusual for the time of the year.

Listening intently he heard the door latch click; then it swung back with a bang. It was opened again and Jane called out:

"Don't be late, Father. It's a bad night. I don't care to be left alone."

"I'll be back in an hour, my lass, and bring Abel Head along with me. He's plenty of time on his hands with these new restrictions in force." It was Tom Thrush's voice; he was going to the Sherwood Inn. What a stroke of luck! Such a chance would not occur again.

Carl Meason chuckled savagely as he heard Tom's footsteps die away in the distance. Creeping out he felt his way back to the motor along the wall, made sure all was right; the lights were low and covered by a dark protection which entirely obliterated them. He had taken every precaution and knew the way in the dark; he had only to keep to the road and get clear away with Jane. Nobody was likely to be motoring on such a night. He was still disguised. He wondered if she would recognize his voice, he could alter it cleverly.

He banged at the door as though he had stumbled against it in the dark. Jane was nervous, more so than she had been since her

142

return. The noise startled her; it could not be her father returning, still there was a chance.

She listened. The knock came again, louder. She opened the cottage door; the light from the lamp shone on the outer door leading to the road.

"Who's there?" she asked, bravely, although her heart quaked.

"I've lost my way. I want to get to Little Trent," said Carl, in a muffled voice.

"Go straight on," she said; "it's not far."

"Who lives here?"

"Thomas Thrush, Captain Chesney's gamekeeper."

"That's lucky; I know him. May I come in for a few minutes? I'm tired."

She hardly knew what to say. If she refused he could force his way in; whoever he was, she thought it better to grant his request; it was a bad night to be out.

She opened the door and Carl stepped through. He walked into the cottage.

"Thanks," he said; "is Mr. Thrush in?"

Jane hesitated a moment; then said:

"He's gone out; he will not be long. You know my father?"

"Quite well."

Something in his appearance was familiar; she looked at him curiously. His eyes fascinated her; they were like a snake's, the eyes of Carl Meason, her husband, as she remembered them to have looked several times. It suddenly occurred to her that he might be her husband disguised; she was almost certain it was. What must she do?

Carl watched her. He caught signs that she recognized him, he had not much time to lose, he must make good use of it and act at once.

"It's me, my lady; I see you know me. Why did you run away from me?" he said.

"What have you come here for in this disguise?" she said.

"To take you away. I am running great risks, but I want you, Jane, and I think you're worth it. You ought to be flattered."

She must parley with him until her father and Abel were at hand.

"I shall not go with you," she said firmly.

"Oh, yes, you will; I think I can persuade you," he said, looking threateningly at her. "You have given me away; that was not proper for a wife."

She said nothing. If only she could detain him.

143

"Come, hurry up. Your father will not be back yet; he's gone to Little Trent, I heard him say so," he said.

"I will not go," said Jane.

"You will, and now. There's your hat and coat. Put them on."

"No!"

He came toward her, looking terrible in his disguise.

"You see this," he said, taking a large knife from his pocket, unsheathing it. "If you do not come at once I will kill you."

She shuddered. She knew he would do it; this was no empty threat. Mechanically she took her hat and cloak and put them on.

"If you cry out I will use it," he said, holding up the knife. She did not speak. He took her by the wrist and led her out; she was not so afraid now, probably it was the safest plan to go with him—she could escape again.

He pulled her rapidly along by the wall until he reached the motor.

"Get in," he said, turning on the small inside lamps.

Jane entered; she heard him fixing the starter; he got in and in a few minutes the car moved.

"It all depends on yourself whether you come out of this alive," he said savagely.

"Where are you going?" she asked.

"Anywhere on to the main road; you can say good-bye to Trent Park, you'll never see it again," he said.

He intended to kill her when it was safe; she felt sure such was his intention. Her faculties were alert. Was there a way out?

Her heart gave a throb, her hopes rose; if she could make him steer a wrong course.

"You are not making for the main road," she said.

"Oh, yes, I am."

"You are not. If you upset the car you may be killed too," said Jane.

He hesitated; she might be right, there were several roads in the Park. He wanted to get away as quickly as possible. He had no head lights; it was safer.

"Which way ought I to go?" he asked.

"More to the left."

Jane knew the ground well; she could find her way in the dark almost as certainly as her father. The car was nearing the road leading past the moat and tower; it was not often used, but he would not be aware of this in the dark.

"To the left?" he said. "There's no road there."

"Yes; a little farther on."

"You can see?" he said in surprise.

144

"I know the park as well in the dark as in the daytime," she answered.

He thought this not improbable; her father had taught her woodcraft, the ways of the forest and the park.

"If you put me wrong you're done for," he said. "You'd better not play tricks with me."

"Why should I when you threaten my life?" she replied quietly.

Her feelings were strung to the highest pitch; she was playing a desperate game. She might lose her life, it was worth the risk. He intended to kill her anyhow because she had given him away.

He thought her thoroughly frightened; she would hardly play him tricks, she dare not. He underestimated her courage.

Jane peered into the blackness; she saw a faint line ahead and knew it was the water in the moat. Her father had taught her to see water in the dark—it comes easy when familiar with nature. Every sense was alert; if she made a mistake he would not hesitate to kill her, for he would know what she had tried to do.

The car jolted. Carl said angrily:

"We're off the road; what's your game? Take care."

"It's all right—a short cut to the main road. That's where you want to go?" she said.

"The main road, yes."

"I'll tell you in a moment; turn sharp to the right then," said Jane.

The car went on. Jane's heart beat fast, her pulses throbbed painfully. Would he do it, would he find out? It was an awful risk to run.

"Now," she said as calmly and steadily as possible, "to the right."

Carl turned the steering wheel; the car swerved, bumped on the rough grass; for a moment he seemed to lose control of it. He heard Jane leap out; he could not see her.

She had played him a trick; where was he? His brain was on fire. He acted like a madman, wild with rage; he tried to stop the car. In his fumbling haste he failed.

There was a plunge, a great splash.

Jane, bruised and shaken on the ground where she had fallen, listened.

145

CHAPTER XXX

NEWS FROM HOME

When Tom Thrush returned home alone—Abel declined to accompany him—he found the doors open, the cottage in darkness, the lamp having been blown out, and Jane gone. He called her, searched the cottage, took his lantern and examined the garden. Somebody, a man, had been there. He went out on to the road, traced footsteps along the wall until he came to where the car had stood, then he knew it was Carl Meason who had carried her off and given them the slip.

Lantern in hand he followed the tracks easily seen in the damp dust covering the road. He walked rapidly. When he came to the turning leading to the moat he stopped and wondered what had taken him this way. A feeling of horror swept over him as he thought Meason might have had an object in taking her to the moat. This vanished when he considered he would not know the way in the dark, but how to account for the tire imprints? He followed them; as he neared the moat he listened. Footsteps drawing near, light treading; not a man, perhaps Jane; if so, what had become of Meason?

It was Jane, moving slowly and painfully. He held up the light.

"What are you doing here, lass? Where is he?" asked Tom.

She stumbled upon him, knocking the lantern from his hand. She had fainted. He laid her gently down and picked up the light, holding it to her face. There was a cut on her forehead; he wiped the blood away, saw it was not serious. She came round quickly. He helped her to her feet.

"How came you here?" he asked.

"Carl came to the cottage. He forced me to go with him. He had a car—he meant to kill me—it was his life or mine," she said, shivering.

"Where is he?" asked Tom.

"In the moat."

He was bewildered, did not understand. Jane could not have pushed him into the water.

She explained hurriedly; he listened wonderingly. She was plucky, had run a great risk. He gave no thought to the man.

"I jumped out and fell on the grass. He seemed to lose his head; the car rushed on—I heard nothing more," she said.

"Then he's in the water and the car too?"

146

"Must be."

"Come home. I'll have a look round in the morning. If he's drowned it's too good for him; he ought to have been hanged. Drowning they say is an easy death."

Jane went to bed and slept the sleep of exhaustion and excitement. She was only a girl and had already gone through startling experiences. Tom, leaving her, went to the moat early. He saw where the car had fallen in; it must have turned upside down and probably Carl was pinned underneath. He felt no compunction; he thought Jane acted rightly. The man was a spy and a villain; she and the country were well rid of him.

When Alan returned he told him what had happened. The matter was reported to the police and to the proper authorities. The moat was searched; it was difficult to drag the car out but it was soon done. Carl Meason's body was found pinned beneath, as Tom anticipated.

The usual inquest was held and strange facts were brought to light. On Meason's body were documents proving he was in the pay of the Germans, and had given much valuable information which was used for raiding purposes.

Jane's conduct was extolled. She would undoubtedly have paid the penalty of betraying his secrets with her life; there was no pity for Carl Meason. He met his death as a traitor; had he been caught he would have undoubtedly been shot.

Jane was searched out and interviewed; Tom made a handsome bargain with the representatives of a Sunday weekly; when she read the account of her life with Carl Meason she was amazed. Had all these things really happened? Was it possible? She pointed out certain extraordinary statements to Tom, saying she did not recollect such things and was quite sure she had told the newspaper man nothing of the sort because they had never happened.

Tom smiled.

"He said he'd write it up, and he has. He's made a good job of it and we've been well paid for it. I think he was entitled to lay it on thick, considering the price paid," he said.

"Did this all really happen to you, Jane?" asked Eve.

"Some of it," replied Jane, smiling.

"And the rest?"

"It is a bit far-fetched; he must have a vivid imagination," said Jane.

Eve laughed.

"You have caused quite a sensation," she said.

Alan went back to general headquarters in France. Eve was as happy as she knew how to be without him, but there was the constant anxiety of what might happen to him.

Alan was not a good correspondent, and he had not much time for writing. Eve knew this and was always glad of a few lines. He came home at intervals for a few days at a time.

Eve loved him and he adored her. Since their marriage he discovered new and surprising traits in her and wondered how he had been so blind as to risk losing her by his delay in asking her to be his wife.

Bernard Hallam and Ella were still at The Forest.

"When am I going back to Australia?" said Mr. Hallam in answer to Alan's question. "I cannot tell you, for I don't know. It's not safe. I have no desire to see how a torpedo works at near quarters. I am much safer here, and The Forest is a delightful place. There's another thing, I want my revenge."

Alan laughed as he said:

"Another couple of races with Rainstorm and Southerly Buster?"

"That's it. They were on a level last time; you only just got home with your pair."

"Bandmaster has probably lost some of his paces," said Alan.

"Didn't look like it when you won the Steeplechase on him," answered Mr. Hallam.

"By Jove, that must have been a race!" exclaimed Alan.

"It was. Don't you recollect much about it?"

"Can't say I do," replied Alan, with a puzzled expression.

"It's funny; you must have been in a queer state."

"I was. I say, Hallam, I believe I went off my head for a bit," said Alan.

"I won't contradict you, but the head's all right now," said Mr. Hallam.

Fred Skane was consulted. He thought Bandmaster quite equal to tackling Rainstorm again, and The Duke doing the same by Southerly Buster. Both would be ready for the next Newmarket meeting if the matches could be included in the program.

Alan communicated with the Jockey Club officials and there was no difficulty about it; the former matches proved such an attraction they were sure to be an addition to the card.

In due course the matches came off and on this occasion honors were divided, for Bandmaster beat Rainstorm, and Southerly Buster beat The Duke. Mr. Hallam would have been more pleased had Rainstorm won, for he was his favorite, but Alan was delighted at Bandmaster's success.

Duncan Fraser was a frequent visitor at Trent Park and always went across to The Forest during his stay.

Eve said she was "watching developments," but Alan laughingly answered that, "Fraser is not a marrying man; he's in love with the brewery, which is much more prosaic."

"We shall see," said Eve; "I'm open to support Ella against business."

Captain Newport, invalided home an exchanged prisoner, came to Trent Park for rest and change. He sorely needed it and Eve looked after him well, also Captain Morby, severely wounded, and several more officers. In fact, Trent Park was turned into a convalescent home, with Eve in command. Ella and some friends were willing helpers, and Jane came every day to do what she could for Mrs. Chesney, to whom she was much attached.

Captain Morby said the man who could not make a recovery at Trent Park was very far gone indeed.

"I say, Newport, I owe you a uniform," said Alan, laughing, and told him how he took his in the house of Jean Baptistine.

"A fine old chap," said Vincent. "He did what he could for me; had I been fit he'd have got me away safely."

"I hear the old fellow's had his place blown about his ears but he's still there. I am trying to smuggle him over here. I'll fix up a small farm for him where he can settle down and try and be contented; I think I can manage it."

"That's good of you," said Vincent.

"Not at all; he deserves it, he risked much to try and save me, he did his best," said Alan.

During Alan's absence in France, Eve had plenty to do at home. The wounded officers took up much of her time. When not attending to them, or delegating the duty to others, she went about the home farm, the stables and the gardens, often visiting Sam Kerridge at the Stud, where Alfonso was doing well and most of the mares were still in possession. Alan's racing establishment had been cut down, but this was not to be wondered at, and Fred Skane had an easier time than usual. Many of the lads had joined up, and more were waiting for the call. Alan generously granted them a portion of their salaries during the time they served.

Eve looked longingly forward to the time when Alan would be free again and live always at Trent Park and where children to be born would increase their happiness tenfold. She wrote him long letters, giving all the news and local gossip, also everything concerning their home. Her latest letter roused Alan's interest more than usual.

"You see, I was right," she wrote; "Duncan Fraser asked Ella

Hallam to be his wife and she consented. I am sure it is a good match, so is Mr. Hallam, and Ella will be happy. Once upon a time I fancied you admired her, I mean were half in love with her, and I am not quite certain yet that she has forgiven me for snatching you away. We were always meant for each other, Alan; it was our destiny, and in this case it has proved very kind.

"And what do you think? Mr. Hallam wants me to sell The Forest to him in order to give it to Ella as a wedding present. Shall I? Tell me. There are many pleasant associations connected with it—the best, that you asked me to be your wife there."

Then followed news which caused Alan to exclaim:

"By Jove, I am glad! I hope it's a boy."

Eve continued:

"And there's something else, another match. Will Kerridge has asked Jane to be his wife; her second matrimonial venture will not be as stormy as her first.

"We are all well here, and my wounded soldiers simply love the place" ("and their nurses," commented Alan, "lucky beggars!").

"I never pass the steeplechase course but it recalls vividly to mind that never-to-be-forgotten day when you won on Bandmaster—the Rider in Khaki."

THE END